The Instinct for Bliss

The Instinct for Bliss

SHORT

STORIES

———— ❦ ————

Melissa Pritchard

Z

ZOLAND BOOKS

Cambridge, Massachusetts

First edition published in 1995 by
Zoland Books
384 Huron Avenue
Cambridge, Massachusetts 02138

Cover image from *A Sense of Mission,* photography by David Wakely,
text by Thomas A. Drain © 1994, published by Chronicle Books.

PUBLISHER'S NOTE
This book is a work of fiction. Names, characters, places, and
incidents are either the product of the author's imagination
or are used fictitiously. Any resemblance to actual events
or persons, living or dead, is entirely coincidental.

FIRST EDITION

Book design by Boskydell Studio

Printed in the United States of America

01 00 99 98 97 96 95   8 7 6 5 4 3 2 1

This book is printed on acid-free paper, and its binding
materials have been chosen for strength and durability.

Library of Congress Cataloging-in-Publication Data

Pritchard, Melissa
The instinct for bliss : short stories / by Melissa Pritchard.
     p.   cm.
ISBN 0-944072-49-6
    I. Title
PS 3566.R578157   1995   94-35507
    813\54 — dc20   CIP

FOR MY DAUGHTERS, NOËLLE AND CAITLIN,
CONCEIVED, IN PART, BY MY OWN
INSTINCT FOR BLISS.

Acknowledgments

For their generous support I thank the Illinois Arts Council and the MFA Writing Program at Vermont College. I am deeply grateful to Pamela Painter, Diane Williams, Dr. Jay Boyer, and Fernando Fernandez, guides who offered insight, courage, and the light to go on.

These stories have previously appeared in the following publications: "Sweet Feed" in *Epoch;* cited in *Best American Short Stories 1990,* Richard Ford, editor. "The Order of Goodness" in *West Branch.* "Closed to the Natural World" in *Hawai'i Review.* "Eating for Theodora" in *STORY.* "El Ojito del Muerto" in *The Southern Review;* anthologized in *Walking the Twilight: Women Writers of the Southwest* (Northland Publishing); cited in *Pushcart Prize XVII* and in *Best of the West 5* (W. W. Norton). "Uriel" in *The American Voice.* "On Faith Alone" in *Denver Quarterly.* "The Good and Faithful Widow" in *The Paris Review.* "Revelations of Child Love" in *The American Voice.* "Hallie: How Love Is Found When the Heart Is Lost" in *The American Voice;* anthologized in *Best of the West 4* (W. W. Norton). "The Erotic Life of Luther Burbank" in *Weber Studies.* "The Instinct for Bliss" in *The Paris Review.*

Contents

The Instinct for Bliss

Sweet Feed

*A little thing comforts us because
a little thing afflicts us.*

— PASCAL

They were cooks, both crazy for food, they could have changed their minds a dozen times.

"What if it was today?"

"Me, I couldn't eat. I could maybe order, but I couldn't get the food down."

"What if he has a heart attack? Fatty dinner, no movement in the cell, stress. What stress!"

"Cooks Become Executioners."

"We'd be heroes."

Bald to the waist, massive as you'd want a cook, Moss had a bland noxious face, spongy hands, arms quivery like puddings when he pounded and cut. He spouted massive sweat, all his various bigness contrasting with a meager, puny attitude to cooking, like it was laundry, a thing he was hired to do. Fifteen years of his kettled cud had saved the prison money, unquestioned. He had no aesthete's eye, no feel for the possibilities, the uses, the salvation of food.

When he got the job, Grady hoped there'd be somebody to discuss cuisine with. He felt conspicuously let down. Moss was a bricklayer, a slabber, misleadingly obese — but what a zero, a collapse, in artistry.

Here it was, now here it came, Waller's Final Supper, with Moss at the dentist for an emergency root canal. He'd kept rolling his stubby finger along his gum yesterday, swearing. Grady knew how Moss intended microwaving Waller's last dinner — a man's final meal on earth — what was more poignant, more deserving of cautious, theologic ceremony? Grady's frustration of the past weeks, ladling splotchy stew, wan bumpy cereals, knifing up pans of nile green Jell-O, his repressed artistry clutched at this opportunity, with Moss home aching in the mouth, to outdo himself. The marketing he could do on his lunch hour; now he should meet Waller, get a better picture of his appetite.

A. B. C. Waller, Jr. had been in prison twenty-two years. He was about to be publicly executed. Waller's disposition, Grady felt, was comprehensible. His own less so.

First he smirked at the mustachio. Waller, a short, average-to-dumpy man, had a freakish mustache waxed out like fancy wrought iron. He diddled and petted alternate sides, spiraling them into horns, except the left side drooped, driving Grady nuts.

Then he started apologetic:

"Sorry to disturb you, Mr. Waller." (From what? contemplating his execution?) "I'm Grady Benson, filling in for the cook who has a toothache, root canal apparently." (Quit babbling . . .)

Grady sipped a breath. "At any rate, I'll be preparing your dinner tonight, so I kind of thought I'd stop by, go over some of the delicate points with you."

Silence.

"I'm something of a professional cook, graduated from cooking school and plan to maybe own a restaurant in five years. I can make you a supper you'll never forget . . ."

Silence.

Grady held up his clipboard. "Moss says you've asked for wild rabbit, black-pepper gravy, twenty buttermilk biscuits, and a blackberry pie. That right, sir?" The voice, since he'd expected silence, jumped him.

"That's right."

"Tricky, the wild part, sir. I can pick up some domestic rabbit over at the butcher shop, if that's acceptable to you."

"No taste to hutch rabbit."

"I could fix a mustard glaze."

"No sauce. Plain fried."

Waller turned. Grady could see his face close. The eyes, so far as Grady could tell, had practically no pupils.

"Rifle shop, somebody'd be likely to get a rabbit for you. They got a different taste, wild. Backyard rabbit's like chicken water."

"I see, thank you." Grady made a note next to wild rabbit — rifle shop, possibly feed store?

He bounced his pencil down the list but Waller shrugged, didn't matter to him, homemade or bakery on the biscuits, if a pie was homemade or store-bought. He was apathetic, enough to cause Grady, with his shopping list, to get frustrated. He would make him care, do up the finest biscuits, pie and pepper gravy Waller'd ever known, and herbs all over the rabbit.

"Well, guess that does it. You ask for milk or coffee?"

"Both."

"No problem. Ah. Pleased to meet you." The silliness of his reflexive politeness stopped him.

Waller, staring between his polished shoes, squinted up as if maybe he regretted Grady's leaving, the visit ending, though he'd acted grudging the whole time. This emboldened Grady, who had a degree of morbid gawker-on.

"Why rabbit, Mr. Waller?"

"Oh hell, probably because of my uncle, him and me used to hunt, he'd cook rabbit right over the fire. Get spin off a wild animal, he'd say. Rub your nose on it, chew on it, you can get tough from its sliding down in you awhile."

The almost primitive poetry, the sadness, Grady couldn't believe it. What he said was "You hunt much before, Mr. Waller?"

"Every season. Some fishing in the summer. I liked it, not killing so much as waiting. Same with the fishing."

"I've had quail before."

"Yeah, quail's good tasting."

"Well, I'd better" — Grady lifted the clipboard — "get started."

Waller'd already turned away, busy with his hair ropes.

Goaded by the man's chilly apathy, Grady took two hours at lunch locating and buying what he needed.

The rabbit was late, making Grady crazy. His blackberry pie with its sparkling, crimped crust sat on the counter. The biscuits, rolled and cut, lay under a damp, striped towel. The rest of the prisoners would still be alive tomorrow; they could get by tonight on cold cuts and packaged cupcakes.

He skimmed the cleaning and jointing instructions; photographs showed yellow hands puppeting before a white drape of apron. The hands sexless, the butcher's apron monolithic. He fretted over the rattan tray, the green linen mat, napkin molded into a fan, the mossed basket of white violets, objects he had borrowed from his own apartment. The rabbit was late, really he should have bought some backyard chicken-water ex–Easter bunny. How could Waller tell the difference?

Then he had his rabbit. "Mature buck," the man from the gun shop classified, letting it sag off his shoulder, drop cloddish onto the stainless steel counter. "Know how to gut?"

Grady was prim. "Of course."

"Hey, this one stood up in the road a bull's-eye on it saying shootme, shootme, help somebody, shootme. Like a darn suicide."

He became grateful time was short; he could have stared at the rabbit a long, grievous while. Chef-like, he angled the shears and jointing knife alongside the plush, puddled body. His cookbook, a large fancy one from England, was propped against the rice canister.

Grady swore. The first photograph showed a hand with shears at a pretty angle slitting the belly, yet the first printed instruction said sever the head at the back of the neck, the feet at the first joint. There was no photograph of a beheading or befooting. He wondered if Waller couldn't be brought in, under guard, to do this first thing. He got the cleaver.

Cupping his left hand over the head and eye like a blessing, he hurled the cleaver in a shuttered motion from his right shoulder. Whack. Where to put the head. Queasy, he balled it up in paper toweling, letting it go with hasty ceremony into the rubber barrel under the counter. He had a hitchcock fear of that head, but one look at the clock sobered him, tethered him to the book's demands. Slit the belly to the vent. He tugged the flesh out from the fur, pulled at the hind legs until they popped loose, severed the tail. In step five, pry front legs free, draw the animal up out of its skin, Grady embarrassed himself by being sick. After hanging over the sink with the taps running, he returned to the skinned carcass, removed the entrails and jointed the body. This was easier. He'd done chickens. It was chicken now, raspberry flesh, the bluish glisten over it. Flipping the pieces in seasoned flour, he began frying them in peanut oil. Good smell, Grady sniffed, thumb-smoothing the white ball of tail, setting it on the ledge, a luck piece.

Two uniformed guards entered the enormous work kitchen while Grady fidgeted with matches and a white candle. Uncover the rabbit last, he told them. Pepper gravy's in this pewter boat. Awarded for his presentations in cooking schools, Grady half-wished for a camera.

"Pretty," one guard said, pinkie in the gravy and sucking.

"Waste of time," said the other.

He'd saved a bit of rabbit for himself on a plastic salad plate. About the time he pictured Waller receiving his meal, Grady

took a small picky bite. He could identify the taste as rank, almost weedy, but couldn't swallow the meat, nipping it out of
his mouth. He began mopping up blood, gristle, sinew.

And later, while Grady was gouging out flubby pale eyes of
potatoes (the cruelties . . . slicing, chopping bits of animal,
mute skinned vegetables — a series of kitchen horrors), one of
the guards returned his tray, the Cynic who'd called Grady's effort a waste. Had it been the other, the appreciative one, he
might have inquired how Waller'd acted, if he'd been pleased.

The two of them, however, both stared at the tray. A blot of
blackberry, a faint swipe around Grady's Wedgwood plate
where one of twenty biscuits had chased gravy. A circle of coffee in the saucer. Knife and fork laid in an X or a cross.

"Why didn't he just inhale the napkin?"

Grady was moved by this ravenous, defiant appetite. He decided to ask.

"Did he say anything?"

"What?"

"Didn't he say something about my dinner?"

"Nope. Just ate."

Grady pictured Waller eating. TV turned down, green napkin
denting into the blue prison shirt. The mustachio, cliché of evil,
bits of food sticking in it. Mouth methodically circling. Aware
of its last bite. Petty, this feeling cheated of a doomed man's
praise, but he wondered if it made a difference (imagine Moss
trying to do that dinner!). Grady's reward would have to be
evidential in the wiped-clean plates and nothing left over.

He carried the tray to the sink, swinging the plate to rinse it. A note lay under the plate. He clunked the plate in the sink, turned off the water, dried his fingers, picked up the note.

It surely is better to step into the next world, tho I doubt there is one, on a full stomach. Rabbit was good, tho not the best. The best is first. P.S. Flowers nice. Yours in All Sincerity, A. B. C. Waller Jr.

"What in hell panty-waist thing is this?" Moss, groggy on painkillers, stared at the tray. "Sonabitch, Grady, this guy's an ice cold killer, a murderer, a no-soul, how come the flowers and doily shit?"

Grady couldn't speak to somebody like Moss about food, its seriousness, how he offered Waller this final vitality of rabbit. Waller's instincts had been perfect, his wish perfect. Grady couldn't explain any of it.

"Why are you back? Your face is still swollen."

"Execution. I could get a place for you."

Now he was staring at the tray. Grady wondered what Moss could be thinking.

"Got an idea for your restaurant."

"What's that?"

"Dead Man's Dinners. You get your menu from a bunch of last suppers. Photos and stories of the guys, what they did, what they ordered. Have people eating in little fake cells."

"Then the check kills them?" Grady snorted, but Moss had turned gray and grumpy so he stopped.

"Great idea, Moss. That is one big idea. Thanks."

"Nothin. Jesus, my face hurts. Feels walked on."

Moss was crammed with the others, face big and hurting watching Waller die. Grady skinned and diced potatoes, then onions, his eyes squeezing water. He couldn't go home. He decided to make sweet dough and freeze it. Five minutes to eleven. Wheeled in on the gurney. Trussed down. Everybody waiting for him to get the injection.

Grady stopped that picture, put in its place a rabbit bounding, springing whole around the woodsy insides of Waller, with violets fragrant, seeding.

In the prison kitchen then, punching gray, greasy dough, in a stink of yeast, Grady brought his forehead to the steel lip of the bowl, wanting comfort from his blind, little rise of bread.

The Order of Goodness

Deception.
The world's not slowing when you, or anybody, falls.
A turning inward like forgiveness.
In the face of all striven-for family order,
What I did was free-willed.
I got tired of gravity.
Got tired, being good.

"Shay? Wake up. Time to get coffee."

He's asleep in the backseat of her station wagon, dirty boots planted in the baby's empty car seat.

"Rise and shine. I've decided you're my nephew."

Shay looks at her sideways, sleepily, the way the Devil might try to deck most women dead. (Oh, he does that, and I want to set fire to those clothes, scrub the first and second layers off him, save him by some wholesome means or otherwise, lie down under him and say go on kill me, take me down to whoever I really am, and another thing, don't stop.)

"Whatever you say, Mrs. S."

She can't get her fill of him, that long, wax-bean yellow hair, black baseball cap, bill turned back, black jeans, boots with chains, black T-shirt, anarchist's scribble, "dead white and blue," peeling off it. Black pencil along the inside rims of his eyes, a silver cross tapped upside down in one nostril. The way he calls her Mrs. S.

Where she finds herself, Indiana farmland, Elkhart County, who wouldn't stare? Anne is driving deeper into this, her reservation confirmed at the Amish farm bed-and-breakfast. When the baby took a small cold, her husband, unselfish to what Anne considered a fault, suggested she go ahead, he'd stay with the baby. It would be good for her, a peaceful trip alone. The neighbor's boy had appeared on her doorstep just as she'd removed the thermometer from inside her sweet baby. A dangerously quiet boy, Anne believed, who needed her ordered, domestic life as much as he relieved the loneliness of hers. Since she'd left her job and stayed home to do exactly what she'd insisted she'd always wanted, take care of a baby, gear down, grow a garden, read more, she had not adjusted, she had subtle fits of panic, stubborn hungers she could not discuss with her husband, who now worked overtime to sustain her wishes, desires now tested, found wanting and inexplicably so. This neighbor boy had taken to visiting sometimes, after school, to baby-sit or to help with chores, and to talk, talk as much as a boy quiet as he was could. Anne listened with sympathy, but now, out of safe context, there was something else.

Bronze-green horse droppings pock the chalky dirt roads. Now and then, they pass a bay horse, hooves spanking muscles glossed with effort, pulling a high-backed black buggy. Shay keeps tally, Cool, Mrs. S., twenty-two buggers.

He figures the gloomy-looking black fringes veiling the horses' necks and heads are purposeful, meant to shoo off flies.

These farmhouses are white, without individuality, without distinction. The gardens, most of them, have scarlet flowers. Velvety cannas, salvias, coxcombs and red hot pokers, what Anne used to consider the ugliest of flowers. The Amish women conceal themselves in long somber dresses and dark bonnets; the men, fully bearded, wear boxy dark blue or black pants and jackets, flat-brimmed straw hats, quaint schoolboys' hats. One farmhouse, one family, one horse and buggy, appear interchangeable with the next, a thing Anne finds aesthetically restful but morally unsettling. The uniformity suggests conservatism, the conservatism implies authority, authority a thing she might submit to or turn defiant in the face of, but could in no way be at peace about.

She slows beside a one-room schoolhouse, white with white rail fencing, a yard of browned grass, a few old-fashioned pieces of play equipment.

"The children stop their education when they turn fourteen. Imagine, if you were Amish, you'd be done already. With school."

Shay likes that. Nobody, he boasts, has ever made him do anything he didn't want to, and there is little, he boasts further, he hasn't done. He looks over at her.

"I called my Mom and told her I'm with a friend. She's working double shifts again, so she's happy I'm somewhere safe. Hey, Mrs. S? Could you pull next to those cornfields? I gotta take a leak."

He breaks from the corn, a scraggly blackbird, comes up to

her car window, holding out a shucked ear of corn, gingerly, as if she were some stray he hoped to tame. Here. Taste. Pressing the corn against her shut mouth until, embarrassed, Anne takes a small bite.

"I never knew corn could taste so sweet."

"You have pretty teeth."

Draining the last of his cherry soda, Shay punches the can under the seat with his boot heel. Anne had panicked, retreated to town, where she bought Shay a soda and a bag of caramel corn. She had a nervous dread of falling and needed to hold back whatever was to happen with some almost maternal gesture.

It is early evening, and Shay has to hang halfway out her car window to see the red-painted letters on the mailbox. H. YODER.

"That's it. Straight down that road."

A white farmhouse, a collar of bare dirt yard.

"Turn that down, Shay, the music. Actually, turn it off please."

Anne has a minor, cold urge to back up, say oh hell we've already tumbled and my fault too, my sin and dishonest doing, let's just get back to town, find a motel and have done with it. Instead, she parks carefully beside an unhitched buggy, and before she can say wait (hold on until I somehow prepare these people for the sight of you), he's out of her car and up the porch steps, chains flashing on his boots.

She talks too fast, covering herself. My husband's home with our little girl, who's sick, he knew it would disappoint me to cancel this reservation, and I hope you won't mind, I've brought my sister's boy, Shay.

These are religious people, they can read straight into her like X ray or judgment. But Mrs. Yoder, her smile perfect as a pin row, says please, come into our home and be welcome. She passes no more than a thumb's glance on Shay.

"We had, you know, set up the room with a double bed for you and your husband. and a crib for the baby. If you would like separate rooms, our boys . . ."

"No thanks," Shay interrupts. "Dibs on the crib, Auntie S."

She laughs, too loudly, curious about a certain profane joy thudding in her chest.

Later, Anne will understand that only strictest breeding kept first Mrs. Yoder, then her husband, from gawking at Shay. Their nine children nudge one another continuously, their faces sweat like dewy berries every time he looks directly at any one of them.

Two of the older boys invite Shay out to the barn, the other children go obedient as ghosts upstairs to bed, while Anne sits with Mr. and Mrs. Yoder in their parlor. On a plain pine table, the opened Bible has a corn leaf wedged along its spine, a marker. There are no other books. No television. No radio. No electricity. No pictures, no window curtains. Some indoor plumbing, she'd heard water running. A house scrubbed of dross. Anne considers her own house, its half-finished projects, baby toys, unread books, thinks of her husband's current virtue, patience. She should go home and throw it all out, shouldn't she, keep only the baby and one plain table with one book on its surface, but what book is that? Unlike Mrs. Yoder, who sits across from her, not much older than herself, Anne, bred for selfishness, for some unspecified distinction, is panicking within the new domestic life she has chosen. A habit of extinction rules her messy house. Mrs. Yoder, eroded, grayed, sacrificed, one of her teeth missing, nine children to Anne's one, looks peacefully surrendered, veiled in serene exhaustion.

These Yoders are slow-spoken, with traces of uneducated or antiquated speech. They know right from wrong to the human marrow. If they are self-righteous, it is a benign stance, for Anne feels purely measured, not judged. There is a deliberate and generous seeding of their God into the folds and gullies of speech and dress. With Mrs. Yoder listening, her hands at rest in her gray, full lap, Mr. Yoder explains the Amish are, above all, a community. Each person as a single grain, is most useless, open to evil, when alone. These precious grains must be ground into one loaf, that Life Bread and Body Jesus tells us is not of this world.

A child comes back downstairs and sits on the couch beside Anne, her white-blond hair peeled into a tiny onion knot. This child regards her gravely, the pointy face, the mild eyes, seemingly clean of all wanting.

With the back of her hand, Mrs. Yoder stifles a small yawn, and Anne, tactful, asks if she might help with the morning's chores. Mr. and Mrs. Yoder look both pleased and amused. Chores, they tell her, begin at four A.M. Oh. Well, I'll try, she laughs, thanks them again, starts up the wood stairs. Her room, they tell her, is at the end of the hall, past other rooms filled with sleeping children.

She opens the door, and what she sees, in the tender spread

of light from a kerosene lamp, is her neighbor's boy, on all fours in the plain crib, singing. He has, he tells her, taken acid. He has, he says, done all this before.

She gets him out to the car (though it's nearly dark, he's wearing her sunglasses) by telling the Yoders, and it was true, she'd forgotten to call her husband, check on the baby.

They drive the four miles to town, down unlit roads with crossings strict as graph points. There is a phone booth beneath a billboard showing a man in a red cap, scaling a gray mountain. GET A GRIP ON LIFE, TURN BACK TO THE BIBLE.

"David? Yes, fine. Just fine. How's Melanie?"

She watches Shay in the car, waving around, talking or singing to himself. Juiced.

"Mmm, you too. What are you doing?" Anne already knows. By the time she gets home, he will have cleaned the house for her, bought roses and a corny card. His predictable goodness. She echoes his kissing noise over the phone and hangs up.

She can't take Shay back to the Yoders'. So she drives for a while on farm roads with bingo names like B2 OR F5. Parks the car, turns off the lights.

"Come on, Shay. Let's take a walk. It's a nice night."

But rural blackness drowns them. There is excess, a terrible load of stars.

They walk down the middle of the dirt road, Shay's arm slopped around her. Anne is having trouble, made anxious by the too-buzzing silence, the militant formations of dry-legged corn, the rustling, penetrable walls on either side of them for darkest miles.

*

They're raised up on their toes, peeking in the schoolhouse window, seeing only their own washed-out faces. With Shay, Anne revolves awhile on the old wheel-go-round. It squeaks as they turn.

When he does kiss her, his mouth is sour and yeasty. Minutes later, he runs and she hears him be sick deep inside rows of corn.

After finding her in the car, he nuzzles his head in her lap while she navigates the becalmed blackness as though at sea. Anne, lost on any number of levels now, by accident comes upon and recognizes the cider mill, the Yoder mailbox, the orchard of apple trees.

A lamp with a note under it has been left burning on the plain kitchen table. The house has Yoder-eyes, God-eyes witnessing, as she persuades Shay, half-pushing his languid body up the stairs.

He is slung forward in the high-sided tub, his back a ribbed plank which she soaps and scrubs. She lathers his hair, digs her fingers in his scalp the way she remembers her mother doing. Clean hurts. Rules protect.

She rubs him dry with a thin green towel, kneeling at his feet like a seamstress. When she stands, his long hair flops against her, wetting her blouse. She makes him use her toothbrush, her toothpaste. She wants him clean, has always wished him this way.

She drapes his jeans and T-shirt across the backs of two chairs, at least she can air them. Turns back the sheet and quilt, coaxing him, pliant, into the square, clean bed. He curls like burning ash. A circle of flesh around his pierced nostril is inflamed, maybe infected.

Anne looks out one window, then another, until he becomes the tenth child in this house, sleeping. A universe of grains, she thinks, each evil and useless, alone. She makes a bed for herself on the floor.

When his weight and voice half-wake her, are on her, she gives in very fast, thinking, Aren't there kinds and kinds, degrees, orders of love?

Anne breathes in the stinging chill of the barn, the rank, wet odor of dung, urine and straw. The Yoders' dog brushes by, black spume of tail popping back and forth, trotting down the clean-swept aisle of the cow barn.

(When she woke to the alarm under her pillow, he was gone, and the kerosene lamp lit so she could see, sitting up, a cross-stitch on the otherwise bare, green wall that said KEEP US TOGETHER IN THE BOND OF LOVE. From the uncurtained hall window, on her way to the bathroom, she saw out to the milking barn, his hand on a cow's black flank, his wax blond hair, and Mr. Yoder, squatted, back to her, milking.)

Now her face wavers, compressed, in the soaking black eyes of cows, one after the other absorbing what she has done with mild, humid blandness. There is the constant splash of urine onto the already brimming, puddled ground.

She comes upon the Yoders' dog, his blunt muzzle worked between the slats of fencing. With immaculate greed, he licks at the stained, rayed disk of a cow's ass. The cow, tail arched, stands in a pure state of sensation. Anne stares at this jointure of dumb bliss, nauseated, strangely consoled. She hears her neighbor's boy at the nearest end of the barn, calling her, and moves into the frame of doorlight.

He cradles her head to his chest, as if she is the child, rubs her hip.

"Mrs. S, this is so cool, I've been up as long as he has" — he nods at Mr. Yoder, approaching with two buckets of grain. Anne unhooks clumsily, stammering, from Shay, who deftly lifts one of the buckets from Mr. Yoder's hand and starts down the aisle. Spinning halfway around to look back at her he says, "Thanks, Auntie S. Bringing me here and all."

Mr. Yoder is looking sternly, she thinks, at her. "Breakfast is ready back at the house," he says, moving past her.

Mrs. S. stands inside a double stall where twin calves lie back to back in a tumbled bed of hay, breathing in an even rise and fall. Above them, a window, a square of glass, a predawn jewel of sky, eye-of-God lapis, lapis of holy parable, Bible, robe. *Doesn't everyone fall, given the chance?* Beneath a clean indigo square, calves breathe, share breath. It is worth cherishing, what they do. Mrs. S. moves out of measurable light or foreseeable distance, drawn by will alone, to do what, Anne could not say, with her neighbor's beautifully quiet boy.

Closed to the Natural World

However opposed their reactions to this natural world, Nadia and Ryan Easton did share and enjoy a derogatory view of middle-class values, never mind being entrenched with three children, suburban home and two cars, in a most prosperous chase of life. They reassured themselves, agreed, and it was sweet, subtle consolation, a kind of binding refrain to their marriage, that they were . . . set apart. They had just come off a convention of Ryan's in Honolulu, each of them drinking more and flirting more than any other time they had attended these annual, vigorous meetings. One woman called her a nymphomaniac, inventive retaliation for Nadia's lukewarm toying with the woman's husband onboard a dinner boat. An alchemy of seasickness, rum punch and Ryan's own blatant flirtations weakened Nadia to the temptation of alluring this unspecial man on whatever brief or shallow level. Oh really, it could have been anyone; perhaps this is what the woman sensed by way of calling her a nymphomaniac.

Nadia considered herself arguably attractive. Her lure, not insubstantial, was wit, a fiercely independent, fertile mind. It was Ryan who was beautiful, though in truth (a phrase he loathed), it was not beauty, in the beginning, fixing, corraling her into this what? — this marriage — but his raw, defiant courting of danger.

Now, cherishing some bohemian ideal, Ryan and Nadia had purchased food, wine, candles, carried them down the steep hill, slick with leaf rot, to their cabin. Without telephone, television or radio, they had three days to themselves on the north coast of Kauai.

There rises in most marriages a tyrannizing familiarity that passes for intimacy, an intimacy grounded in habit, the habit falsely presuming permanence. Nadia and Ryan were comfortable — comfortable within assumptions, their marriage decent because there were no crises, nearly everything meshed smoothly, including the lower gears of their most unremarked selves.

Nadia's primary response to the verdant, drippy lushness of this remote spot was anxiety. She rushed herself through unpacking food, hanging up clothing, checking light switches, thumbing through books, tossing a hyped-up chatter in Ryan's direction. The silence so unsilent, muggy with the threat and breath of vegetation, the dense pitch of birds, unnerved her. Ryan was instantly at home, stripping down to shorts, seizing a walking stick and setting down the rock-bordered path to the sea. Nadia, glad he'd gone, needed little, vain, calm things to do — fix her makeup, brush her teeth, wander about her new confinement until she felt, however tentatively, like stepping onto the porch. She was a little hurt he hadn't wanted to make love immediately as he once would have, in a place as exotic as this, that his initial impulse was to explore not her, but the unknown. She anxiously checked the mirror for offense

(years later, Nadia would learn of Ryan's infatuation with another woman, an unrequited, addictive preoccupation, explaining his current coolness, which she wrongly and naively blamed on herself.)

Braver now, she walked down the path, overgrown and thickly fragrant with yellow and red hibiscus, coconut and banana trees. The earth was springy with wet mold; on her right, a stream of freshwater pushed toward the sea. The path was dark-canopied, humid; she reached with relief the open beach, the hot sun, and at this time of afternoon, the still flattened thinnish sea.

Nadia did not, until shading her eyes, see her husband, a spidery bleakness atop some rocky cliffs far down the beach. Around her, scattered like an enormous, stolid tumble of briquettes, were pumiced volcanic rocks. She had begun to pick her way up a black mountain of them when something scuttled damply over her bare foot. She yelped, leaping back from a dull black crab. The rocks bulged with them, hundreds in weird camouflage. Retreating to a shaded area beneath some palms, she sat against an overturned, peeled and rotted rowboat. Nadia employed nature, liked having it as reference to draw analogy from, but shrank from its active terror and challenge. She might pretend to relax in its presence, never would she lower her mental guard or be insensitive to its peril.

Ryan strode, the one possible word, strode up the soft yellow sand stretch, finding her where he'd expected. They sat together, she confided her fear of the awful crabs, he laughed, said he'd had fun, playing with them.

They hiked the path to the cabin, did make love, the setting rendering them almost new to one another, though Nadia noted, as she usually did, how Ryan kept his eyes closed tight to her, saying nothing, concentrating on her pleasure, which she felt obliged to present him before he would take his own. In this regard, he was a generous, expert lover, yet, today, her mind and emotions remained untouched, a thing he did not know.

They sat on the porch at sunset, drinking wine, discussing whether to go into town for dinner or have a fire on the beach, go to bed early. They decided on the fire, Ryan having already fashioned one from dry, brittle palm fronds.

Their fire was small between the twin lengths of black, empty beach. A couple of cats, lank and gray as pipes, materialized, banging their sides against them. Ryan wouldn't touch the cats because of fleas, lice, rash, but Nadia did, deliberately scratching their stony, gnarled heads. Ryan talked so little, whenever a gap felt too wide or too scary, she noticed how deftly, convulsively, she brought up the children, that bond between them, so tensile and emotionally loaded. The girls were in Honolulu with her parents, who lived in a condominium, being well-spoiled with trips to the beach, the swimming pool, McDonald's.

Nadia sat cross-legged, the fire before her, questioning if there wasn't some transcendent lesson in nature, some moral casting of oneself into Sojourner, some sense of probable catastrophe beneath the symmetry and clarity and vastness; these were her thoughts when Ryan announced that in the morning they would snorkel, out there — he gestured with casual generosity — to the wide cove spread before them.

Without a guide? By ourselves? she asked. At the convention, Nadia had tried snorkeling with a group of unpracticed women — had been the one grabbing onto a rope buoy tied to the instructor's waist, her panic uncurbed. Ryan and one of the other men, warned of dangerous currents, had swum out to a distant reef to view a nest (was that the term, *nest?*) of sea turtles. Nadia had taken such pride, going out at all, pelting frozen peas into ravenous swarms of fish, for her this had entailed anxious surrender. That's nice, Ryan head-patted her. Good effort, dear; she'd hated his belittling of her courage. Now he expected her to accompany him, unguided, into private reefs, deserted seas. She concealed from him her dread of the morning and its ordained activity. Maybe it would rain, a hurricane would blow in or she would be ill.

Ryan served breakfast on the damp porch — papaya, banana bread, yogurt, coffee. He was darkening to rum color, his eyes a hero's improbable aquamarine. Oh why did his beauty, set off by this filigreed lushness, intimidate her? Why should it? She felt out of her territory altogether, her own skin pale, prickling with heat rash. She had given up makeup, felt vulnerable and exposed, though Ryan assured her she looked younger, healthier.

The day was calm, hot. She followed him down to the beach, watched him in the sea, already yards out by the time she spit into her mask, rinsed it in the salt water, tugged it over her head. Water slapped across her belly and legs and shoulders; wide-eyed, face down in marbled, pale green water, her breath harsh as factory machinery. A wedge of silvery, needle-nosed fish, like scores of floating pliers, zipped under her face. The cartoonish sight shocked her into confidence, she started pushing with her arms through supple water, seeing the fish everywhere. Distracted from panic, for whole minutes she imagined herself equal to Ryan, another sort of person, athletic, brave, pioneering. She trailed him onto a tan-pink shallow reef where black urchins stuck up everywhere, quilled and menacing. She was forced to steer with her fingertips over sharp coral, sucking her stomach up to her spine to avoid cutting herself or bumping against black quills. Both of them were suspended in only a few inches of water. He signaled to her, exhilarated. She signaled back, drained. A typical pattern, though he would be gracious, never reveal that he was disappointed in her, though how could he not be, just as she regretted his inability to hear poetry without impatience, without looking flatly bored?

Afterward, as compensation or balance, they hiked out of the valley, drove into town. They rented bicycles, then Ryan rented a surfboard, trying unsuccessfully to surf as she watched. They had dinner, paid for an exorbitantly expensive view of the sea. A little drunkenly, they groped, stumbling down the steep dirt hill to their cabin, navigating by no moon and a weak aura of stars.

On the last day, Nadia began to enjoy the quiet in her body, the levels of civilized tension draining off her. She felt lovely, in some way integrated. Her hair had gone quite wild, bushy with humidity, her face was plain, didn't mirror the loveliness she felt. Ryan looked more and more, for god's sakes, like a movie star, his indifference to this for some reason paining her. Perhaps she wanted vanity to mar him.

They read until noon, then walked to the beach. Ryan removed his shorts, walking naked, with Blake's easy innocence. Nadia, straightening up from retrieving two perfect shells, the first unbroken ones she had found, was first to see someone approach, it seemed to her a young boy, whose wave she returned tentatively.

The boy turned out to be a young woman with cropped hair, her small bare breasts as darkly browned as the rest of her. She wore only the printed bottom half of a bikini. Calmly, Ryan pulled on his shorts.

She stood before them, perfectly vital, her small breasts like gifts of breathtaking honesty. Nadia, wanting to look hard at those beautiful, warm, truthful breasts, politely overfocused on the girl's face and wondered where Ryan was looking. The girl accompanied them up the path to their cabin, drank a glass of orange juice, answered what were all Nadia's questions. She had come from Tennessee to be a cook in a Girl Scout camp, ended up here, on Kauai, camping alone in her tent, exploring the island. She had lived this way a year and a half. She had no other plans.

Oh wow, these two shells are pretty. Uh-oh.

What?

Did you pick them out of the water, off the reef? They're still alive.

Nadia looked. Tiny bluish lobsters, winding out of the perfect shells, waving dark blue clenched nippers.

Want me to put them back for you? You wouldn't want them to die, just for souvenirs, right?

I guess. But Nadia was disappointed. She had wanted souvenirs.

The girl didn't stay long, but afterward, the cabin seemed transformed, she'd left some jolting energy in the room.

Nadia's opened poetry book, Ryan's eyeglasses on the table, so carefully placed, their proud attempts to temporarily disown the middle class, seemed so — middle class — the trail back so clear, the car parked up the hill, the house in its suburb, the money in the bank.

Nadia was sure Ryan must be madly stirred on all levels of attraction for such a disturbing, freed vision of woman. Free from attachment, from fear, athletic (god, she even hunted her own fish), surely any man's dream.

Didn't you love her? Nadia burst out, mainly because she had and could not confess it.

Not especially. I figured she was a lesbian. If anything, she loved you.

Nadia was startled. What?

She talked to you the whole time, looked at you. I was invisible, I didn't exist. Look, she forgot to take your little victims, your souvenirs, back down to the beach.

They joked awhile about her, admired things about her, worried over her safety, agreed neither of them could live the way she did (though Nadia did not entirely believe Ryan's disinterest). Then Ryan decided to go snorkeling a last time, but she could not bear the idea, could not conquer all those fears again. He went alone, she went to sleep.

When Nadia awoke, the cabin was nearly dark, hours had passed and Ryan was not back. Oh god, he drowned. I was too much of a coward to go with him, now he's dead, I killed him, my stupid cowardice killed him.

She scrambled, slid in sleepy panic down the path, nicking her ankle on a rock. She was furious at his damn confidence in himself. She would have to raise the children alone, face everything alone. Yet at some cool core of her angry panic, Nadia felt odd relief, an oasis, as if widowhood might be equated with profound release, a place of retreat from this reckless husband.

She wrenched the same ankle she'd nicked, stumbling down the beach, facing the sea's hard horizon, its setting sun. She scanned both directions, did not see him. The isolation of the beach, the complacent slap of water enraged her. Where was he? She feared the world's beauty, as she feared her husband's. What had she counted on, what had she married, his courage?

Nadia.

Her husband reclined, naked, in magazine posture, against the overturned, rotting boat. The treacherous disappointment she felt, seeing him safe, was immediately eclipsed by a wide, ordinary gratitude.

Oh Ryan, god. She clapped her hands foolishly, like her grandmother, over her chest. I really am so stupid. I thought you were dead.

Never that easy, he smiled.

A statement prophetic and true as their sex that night, the bluish lobsters caught in a wineglass beside the bed, condemned within their faultless shells, while Ryan and Nadia Easton, distant from the natural world, closed their eyes to one another.

Eating for Theodora

Her mother leans across, snaps open the car door.

"Where were you? I'm late again."

"Swimming."

She gets in the car, its white leather smelling sharp, new. Her stepfather is a credit-card daddy, buying cars, furniture, vacations. Hah. Picked her mother up dirt-cheap.

"I haven't time to drop you home, you'll have to come to class with me. Here's an apple and cheese. Eat. God, you're thin again."

Back pressed to the wall, Toni watches an aerobics class of elegant, sweating women. Her mother is appallingly beautiful, a fact Toni is impatient with, the unfair effect it has on men, women, and less noticeably, children. Her mother's defiant ambition is to preserve her looks. It used to make Toni desperate; she would ache for the new wrinkle, the thinning in the neck. Now she hunkers, in military boots, ripped jeans and a fuchsia T-shirt that says, "NUCLEAR WAR? THERE GOES MY CAREER!" her dark hair cropped above one ear, past her chin on the other side, magenta crisscrossing the top. She's observed these ladies for some twenty minutes, taking one chomp of apple, the pulp in her mouth, a contaminant, gushy brown. Cheese slices stick in a little bag on her thigh, melting tiles. She feels sick, chlorine fumes off her damp hair and skin keep her from throwing up. Her mother winks at her from the front row.

Toni leaves to find the bathroom, spits the pulp into the toilet, abandons the apple, the cheese, on the sink. No one expects less from this world. She gluts on air, her own breathing stuffs her.

Her mother drives them home, past houses Georgian or Tudor, imitation Frank Lloyd Wright, trees linked and stately, lawns vast and immaculate. There is cold distance, a dark iris of privacy surrounding this pale, almost divine wealth.

"How was school?"

"Okay."

"Just okay?"

"Yeah, it was okay."

Her mother, Clarice, tilts her wrist prettily to read her new watch.

"Oh, sweetie, I've got decorating class tonight. Would you fix us a couple of Lean Cuisiners so I can shower real quick? Those chicken whatsits, Marsalas, are decent, let's have those."

Clarice has a boyfriend, a lover, for whom the decorating class, they both understand, is a euphemism. This boyfriend recently gave her a sweater, an ugly sweater, which Clarice waved at Toni, thinking they would be like girlfriends, make fun, have hysterics.

"Do you have homework?"

"Sort of. We're reading about the War of the Roses."

"Wow. I remember that. Studying that."

Her mother snaps out the Sting tape, takes it in the house while Toni goes out to see the pool, calm herself, think about being underwater. Anytime.

With a wooden spoon, she keeps the plastic bags of chicken Marsala and rice pinned under boiling water. With effort, she manages to slit the hot plastic, squeeze sweet, wet chicken into two bowls. Her mother appears, in the boyfriend's ugly sweater, her hair sexily mussed, her makeup borderline vulgar. She pours a glass of low-calorie wine.

"Gee whiz, Antonia, I dis-like intensely that mah-roon hair. You had, have, such pretty hair. I wish I didn't have to work out and could stay half as thin as you. You're too thin again. Your bones are seesawing straight through your skin."

They're at the kitchen table having this meal neither of them especially wants, when the phone rings, and Toni gets it. "It's Daddy."

"Raymond? You mean Ray?"

Raymond is Toni's father; since the divorce, he's lived in New Mexico, and according to Clarice, has gone eccentric, totally bizarre.

"Oh lord, what can he want? I'll take it upstairs."

Her mother returns to the kitchen just as Toni's done trashing her Marsala down the disposal.

"He wants you to come out for the summer. I thought we'd planned summer school. God knows what sort of *dump* he lives in, who his friends are. I bet he has at least one girl-friend."

"Mom, I want to go."

Total piece of cake. All her mother has to do is figure how much more time she'll have with her boyfriend. Clarice is like one of those library books with extrahuge type.

"Honey, let's discuss later. I'm super late. Eat a bowl or two of ice cream, something fattening, promise? I'll be home about eleven. If anybody calls, I'm at decorating. Thanks, sweetie."

In the pool, the dirt and drag of this world cannot master her. In water green and chlorinate, she drums through softening rib cages of saints, their faces dolorous, ivoried beads. Her flesh works, diminishes; they swarm, feeding.

Late, from her window, from behind curtains, she sees Clarice and this younger man in the water, legs wrapped around one another, her mother shh, shh, laughing, probably drunk, fooling she's a girl. The water bulky as tar, the saints put away.

In her striped bathroom, Laura Ashley–striped to match her bedroom, all her mother's pink and white controlling, she razors her bangs in a V over her eyes, nudges the scale out of the closet, mounts it like a guillotine. No breakfast, skip lunch, sixty laps at the pool.

She hasn't seen Raymond in five years, not one picture. Clarice, who has, will only declare he looks bizarro (if he wants to be a pathetic, aging hippie, fine by her). So when Toni gets off the bus at ten o'clock at night to wait primly beside her luggage in front of the tiny Taos station, she expects to have difficulty recognizing her father, she doesn't anticipate his utter absence. After ten minutes, she's panicked, thinking taxis, motels, the next bus to the airport, a pay phone but Raymond doesn't have a number, he doesn't even own a telephone; she's still panicking when an old black pickup with a face like Pluto bounces up, two people inside and two identical dogs wagging tails in the back.

Raymond is short, stringy; under streetlight she sees jeans, cowboy boots spackled with mud, hair in a flat, toad brown ponytail to his waist. Toni ducks her head around to see who's left in the truck. A girl.

"Toni. Holy shit. Great to see you. *Tapestry* suitcases? Your mother's remained her socially hauling-ass self. I'll put these bourgeois embarrassments in the back of the truck so they'll get thrashed sooner than later . . . what are those, red stripes in your hair? All right."

"Who's that?"

"Who's who?"

"In the truck."

"Oh. Amalia. She's been helping me clean. She's probably your age. How old are you?"

"Fifteen."

"Godbless. I remember fifteen."

Toni's scrunched between them, between her father and this Spanish girl, Amalia, who's so plump and perfumed it gives Toni nervous nausea. Ray grinds the gears like hamburger, punches into the street as if he's pissed, which he isn't, it's how he drives.

"Hungry? McDonald's is all that's open."

Toni's no is reflexive, Amalia's soft, tempted. Toni feels her appraisal, taking in the postpunk haircut, the black ankle-length dress and ballet slippers. Toni has invested her clothing allowance in black, it has the advantage of being both worldly and occult. In black from her wrists to her ankles, no one can tell how thin she is. People have to consider its slimming effect.

Raymond follows the main road through town, turns, turns again, bounces into a gullied dirt area in front of a long, mint green warehouse that says ANGLADA'S BUILDING — it looks to Toni like a funky auto garage.

"You live here?"

"Ho, Miss Snarky Remark" — Raymond's grinning — "we've been cleaning all day. Maybe not what you're accustomed to, but it's been sweet home for some time now."

Half of Anglada's (Raymond has no clue about Anglada) is a dilapidated roller rink; on Fridays, one guy rents it, skates around for hours by himself. Without music.

To get to the rest of the old adobe building you have to push through molting drapes, red velvet stage curtains, to locate Raymond among his stinky jumble of oddities, old carousel figures, sculptures from jar lids and coat hangers, green elk antlers, scuzzy pelts, old bicycle parts, busted tepees Ray scavenges for sale or trade. The place has a hallucinogenic flow, claustrophobic, entangled, liberating. There is this space of Raymond's, a closet-size kitchen with a woodstove, rickety blue table chairs, then Toni's room, a wood crucifix on one wall, an iron bed with a shredding blue quilt, a small corner fireplace. Raymond thunks her suitcases down, shows her a leather trunk at the foot of the bed. The single deep-set window has a mayonnaise jar stuffed with fat roses. The dogs trail Raymond slavishly, scratching the linoleum floors. Borzoi wolfhounds he got in exchange for a dentist's chair. *Très* weird animals, high, flat, dimensionless. Like they got squeezed in one of those flower presses, Toni says. Pressed dogs.

"Yeah, they bark flat, come to think of it. Amalia brought these roses from her grandmother's garden, right out that window" — Raymond points — "about fifty feet away. Sweet old lady, Theodora. So how's your mother?"

"Okay, I guess."

"She says you're having trouble eating again?"

"For a while. Not anymore. I feel fine."

"Well, that counts. How about some ginseng tea and fortune-less cookies? This bag I got, so far all the little papers are blank."

She watches Raymond two-step around his kitchen; he has a spot, a large, moist freckle, laid into the white of one eye, his ponytail is cinched by a piece of leather, his teeth are tobacco stained. He wears a wide silver concha belt. In a million years and for a million reasons, she cannot picture him with her mother. Last time she saw him was at a wedding. He'd worn a white tuxedo and let her dance the old funny way, her feet parked on top of his. She'd been a baby when Raymond and her mother divorced, and Clarice refused to discuss it. An error, she'd say. A tragic, Shakespearean error on my part.

"Is there a pool in town?"

"Yup, indoors. You can walk or ride my bike. You like swimming?"

"Pretty much. Can I go tomorrow?"

"Hey, babe, it's your summer, go for it."

Toni takes Raymond's old mountain bike down parched, serpentine roads, past cattle blotched in alfalfa like sullen flies. Downtown, in the Spanish-style plaza, she walks the bike, navigates through tourists, following Raymond's directions. Coming in from dry glare and pinkish dust, she feels she has slid under a rock, into this dark, indoor pool smell, green light, heavy chlorine odor. The water long and turquoise, the pool blank. In the dressing room, Toni takes off her black pants, the wrist-length Chinese blouse. Her suit's solid white except for Minnie Mouse waving pink daisies across the butt, one of her fat, red shoes kicking up. Toni relies on mirrors to tell her things, keeps two in her purse, pulling one or the other out to affirm some piece of herself, her earthly presence. In a full-length mirror, she sees her upper arm is bony, like an animal's, spooky and flat from the back then dipping in, getting tiny, some shank a dog might worry. She walks out, paying her dollar to swim, liking the way the Spanish boy stares, fascinated then withdrawn . . . she likes dominating his field of curiosity, inviolate.

The pool is warm, a summer pond. Her contact lenses are out, everything has lost clarity but water, where life is complex and about survival, surviving through motion, through the repetitive motion of swimming. Her arms row, pulling the root of her body, water breaking in through her ears, into the center of her head like glassy splinterings, water dressing the surfaces of her opened eyes. Long black T's wobble and shake along the bottom of the pool, she increases her stroke to the speed where she is a bird, arms winging, elbows cocked; when she raises her head, rainbows haze the windows and doors, the Spanish boy who guards her. Colors of oil slick radiate from the doors and windows, from the Spanish boy, who sits, silent and dry.

Later, she bikes to the library, an old rambling adobe with turquoise doors and windows, flagstone porches with treelike sprays of pink geranium. She finds *Lives of the Saints* in the reference room, sneaks it into her big straw purse, not theft, no — she'll return it someday.

On the way back to Anglada's, Toni stops for cappuccino and biscochitos, local cookies spiced with anise. In a court-yard, on a canary yellow chair, its legs half-sunk in gravel, her book of saints opened, the sun like heretical fire on its print, Toni feels guilty, eating, feels the fat filling her shoes, bunching up her legs, how bloated she is, out of whack from these cook-ies whose taste takes her power, the anise hypnotic, rolling over her tongue, up the sides of her mouth like wine. To pun-ish herself, she rides past Anglada's up a long, unshaded incline and back down, though her legs are weakening and she is on a current, an eddy of exhaustion so profound she is weightless and the cars mirages, honking, wavering like the black T's in the pool. She practically lunges into the cramped interior of Anglada's, escaping the thorny glare of outside. Raymond has gone off to one of his girlfriends', leaving her a note to pick up their laundry at Amalia's, along with five dollars to pay the grandmother for the use of her machines.

The lady opening the door is skinny, dark and sour; sponge curlers bunch like pink fruits on her head; behind her, a washer thrashes, chugs, presumably with their clothes.

"I'm Antonia, Raymond's daughter? He asked me to pay for our laundry."

"Yes, come in. It isn't finished yet."

"Are you Theodora?"

"No, no, one of her daughters. Come in. We're cleaning from lunch."

Toni has never stood in a house this small and, by Clarice's standards, this poor, (migawd, she hears her mother). But there is a scrubbed cleanness, a sense of objects honored for plain utility. The kitchen has canary yellow walls, copper pans lined up, red geraniums profusely clouding windows, yet Toni feels purity covering heartbreak, some persistent sadness darkening, however invisibly, this house.

A woman with a square, jowled face stands up from a red Formica table.

"Sit. Sit down."

The daughter rinses a sinkful of dishes, Theodora closes her crossword book, and Toni sits.

"Would you like an empanada? We baked this morning."

"I'm not sure. What's an empanada?"

"Pastry with meat, spices, raisins."

"Sure. *Gracias.*" Toni grins. "Whatever."

This first time, meeting Theodora, so many people come and go from the small house, aunts, uncles, daughters-in-law, cousins. She thinks of her mother's house, enormous, decorated with expensive, untouched objects. How no one is ever there.

Amalia and her boyfriend have their arms around each other's waists, staying to one side of the refrigerator so the grandmother can't see the boy with his black, curling hair and thick, polished arms sending his hands squeezing around Amalia's butt. After a while, they take the aunt for groceries. Theodora still sits with Toni, who has not touched the empanada, maybe an insult, a waste of food, so she raises it to her mouth and scrapes a few flakes of browned pastry off with her teeth. Its flavor intrigues, repels her; then she sees Theodora's hands tremor, she looks up to see grief blunting her face, and Theodora drying her cheeks with a dull punching of one fist. What has she done? Has she done anything wrong?

"What?" Toni asks, apprehensive.

"No, not you. It's not you."

Silence, weighted, alarming, swerves the chemistry in the room.

"Not you . . . it's my sadness. My husband was murdered."

The empanada turns to weight in her hand, homely, greasy.

"Oh, God. I'm sorry."

"Shot to death. Here." She places her hand against her chest. "This is how I see angels. Five years now."

Telling, she cries. Toni wants to but has not known raw, traumatic loss. She begins to understand the desperate work, the compulsive scouring of household objects.

They sit, the clock ticking over the sink like water dripping. Toni accepts the napkin Theodora passes, done with talking, done crying, her face almost quiet.

"You are too thin for such a young girl."

Toni brushes her lips with the napkin, ashamed.

"I was ill. I lost a lot of weight."

"The Devil helps himself when you are weak, finds his way into you. Do you eat now that you are better?"

"Yes," Toni lies. "I do. The empanada was very good."

"No, you haven't touched it."

Toni takes an apologetic bite. It stops in her mouth, at the back of her throat.

"I believe in angels," Toni confesses, swallowing. Why is she saying this? Why? "Woah. I've never told anybody that. I mean *nobody* knows what I believe."

"Of course. Angels are always present with God. But the man who took my husband's life is out of prison, I pray God finds him, this man." Theodora rubs her hands down her thighs. "I pray for it, then feel bad about this hate in me. Five years of this hate."

In the little squared flower garden, Toni shifts the laundry basket from stomach to hip. Theodora, pulling up weeds, piling them in wilted heaps, moves with the immodesty of those with no one to please, in dark baggy pants, a print smock, her face stern, pulled down. In Theodora's presence, around her lack of vanity, Toni feels strangely calm, as if she can almost breathe. She thinks of her mother's anxious self-absorption, of her father's string of girlfriends. Toni has met three since she got here; there are, he says, several more. Raymond is often gone, coming in at unpredictable times, in unpredictable moods.

"I was born in this house, my father, too. I've been here seventy-five years. I can remember when Doctor Cetrulo was the only person in town with an automobile. Now people are in a hurry to get I don't know where."

"I starve myself."

"Anyone can see you have chosen to do this. To be angry in this way."

"I think I'm trying to be like the saints, like the angels. The less I take from life, the closer I can be to God."

Theodora seizes the grasshoppers off the rosebushes, one at a time, squashes them inside her fist.

"The one you're hurting is yourself, not the world. This is taking, this starving, and God wants us to give, Antonia. Don't you think I asked for death back then, waited for death like a young woman wanting her husband at night, again and again? No. God puts us here to give. No matter how it hurts."

Toni swims, rides Raymond's bike around, visits Theodora. Fridays, she sees the therapist, a thing Raymond and Clarice agreed on — if Toni visits, she has to See Someone.

"When was your last menstrual period?"

"I don't remember."

"Six months, a year?"

"I don't remember."

"Antonia, you're uncomfortable with the idea of sex, with yourself as a sexual person?"

"I'm not a sexual person."

"What about love?"

"I love God."

"Have you been getting along with your father?"

"He's pretty cool. He doesn't try to change me."

"Have you met anyone here you especially like? Are close to?"

"No."

The therapist works with Toni's addiction to swimming, her lapses of timesense, how she plays with food, manipulates it, punishes herself for putting anything in her mouth. These sessions are predictable, narrow in scope. Toni passes reassurance to this therapist like salt, promising to eat, confessing misplaced pride, denying her flesh.

It is only in the long, yellow kitchen, the flower garden, the dark, lilac-smelling bedroom with its rosaries, pictures of Jesus, the Pope, the saints, that Toni breathes and begins to eat, tomatoes from a neighbor's garden, mountain raspberries, mostly for Theodora, who feeds her, insistent, nourishing.

Theodora asks Amalia to drive them to Chimayo, to the santuario, saying it will do them all good. Amalia borrows her uncle's blue Ford truck with the rosary wrapped around the radio dials, and with the three of them lined up in the cab, Toni studies their hands, Amalia's plump and brown with oval, sugary nails, Theo's roots, puffed and dark, her own hands, limp and freckled, tentative. This drive through mountains is long. Toni feels a certain panic, hurtling through mountains too immense, indifferent. Relentless rollings of pine and piñon, tough, uncompromising sunlight she cannot get used to, timelessness, a disorientation; she has never swum in open water, never entered water with no graspable boundary, always kept to pools with hard defined edges that could save her. These mountains have a maniacal open-endedness, a grandiose power over the human and the weak. They devour her.

Then the road curves, drops until they enter a valley of orchards, pastures with cattle, sheep, black and chestnut horses. Amalia turns down a dirt lane shaded by arching cottonwoods

with heart-shaped leaves; on Toni's side, water pushes slug-
gishly through an irrigation ditch choked with red willow.

Getting down from the truck, she follows Amalia and
Theodora across a gray, warped footbridge into an adobe-
walled courtyard with tall, conical evergreens, a flagstone floor
with gravestones, a skinny wood cross. Toni enters the dark,
empty santuario, imitates Amalia and Theodora, tracing a
cross on her face with sour-smelling holy water.

To pass from the linen mildness of summer, the heart-leaves
of old cottonwoods, air gold, solid with roses, to enter a place
rough as a cave, formed out of mud and wood and trapped air,
lit by candles, watery white ovals with charred wicks, hundreds, each a misery or supplication, two deep-set windows
pulling in sparse, lavender light, this is divine, intended assault
on the deadened human spirit. Theodora crosses herself twice
with holy water, her sandals slapping up her bare heels, down
on the reddish stone floor. She and Toni sit on a wood bench
near the altar, in dimness like cloth, in cloying, waxen heat.
The altar has a gilt screen with primitive figures in faded
cobalt, faded ocher, worn gold, Christ centered between
painted curtains, a puppet theater, the puppet on a dark green
cross. Doll figures sit on either side of the altar, a blond, curly
haired boy in a pink satin dress and gold crown, an arrow-
faced man on a starved horse in a glass case. When she looks to
the side, Toni's heart does a fish-jump. A second wood panel,
this with ocher and black warrior-angels and apostles and at
its center, a carved life-size man in an ivory satin robe with
gold trim, hands X-ed, ribs leaking red, his large, almond eyes
black-rimmed, Egyptian-looking.

A terrible sensuality thickens the air in this plain Spanish church. Toni, kneeling, stares through laced hands. Theodora prays, rubs her swollen knees. When Amalia goes up to the altar, and stoops through a little door on the left, Toni and Theodora get up to follow her.

In a dark, thin room, stifled in sweet warmth from tiers of lighted candles, she ducks her head through a second warped doorway, enters a second, tiny room where the cement floor has an open circle of dirt. Theodora kneels, pushes her pained fingers in this dirt. Toni trails hers, too, in cool siltiness, crossing herself. A window with an iron grill lets in a hard block of light — Toni sees horses ripping alfalfa, is conscious of the bright constancy of birds, sees the world green and golden. But God is here, dark, thick-smelling, pressed liquor, dressed up in dolls, put into amateur paintings and plastic flowers, a glass box with Jesus in there on a black cross, in a pale satin gown, the reins of a rosary on his wilted neck. Snapshots of infants, children, families, couples, all Hispanic; a man, naked, reclining in bed, laughing, his black mustache shiny and potent, for what reason, pinned under the tendriled legs of a small crucified Jesus.

She walks back to the first room, one wall solid with crutches, canes, orthopedic shoes, names and dates scratched or inked on them. A handmade white chapel, inside a baby king in a rose satin dress, baby shoes curling around his tiny, chipped feet, a broken basket with three pennies. The other walls, floor to ceiling with oil paintings, velvet paintings, pictures made from sequins, gold and red glitter, carvings from cedar, sculptures from tin, of Jesus, Mary, the saints, so many bloodied submissive Christs — and everywhere letters, photographs, testimonies of souls, tributes of the healed, prayers for the dead, the murdered, the missing, the failed. The wavering heat, perfumed stench from hundreds of candles, the dozens of doll-holies in pastel gowns, beads, plastic roses, and Our Lady of Sorrows, long in black, face behind veils, body sealed in an opaque plastic bag, intercessor for sorrow, hanging in one dark comer.

Theodora and Amalia have gone. She studies every picture, reads every letter, in its smeary pencil or perfect ink, in its Spanish or English, some words misspelt, all put down with painful effort. Bloodied wings flash out of her head, angels pack the place, tread the walls and air with holiness, made giant by humility and stark belief in magic, in idolatry, in baby shoes set before a little red-mouthed doll with yellow hair. Such gothic naïveté is Truth to her, Grace to her, serving the ache to be released.

At the end of the dark aisle, wood doors slope open to the glaring courtyard. She finds Theodora and Amalia at a picnic table drinking Cokes, talking in Spanish, laughing. How did they so easily reenter the world? Toni may never speak again, or it will be tongues and babble, for God is all over and in her body, swarming, His wings clap her face, deafening.

Amalia, seeing her, waves.

"Hey, Toni. I need to use the rest room. Come with me. Eeei, I thought I was pregnant for sures. Then I prayed and took some of that dirt and guess what, sitting out there with my grandma, I felt the blood starting to come."

Amalia is beautiful, glazed with sexuality, fertility; if she is not pregnant now, surely she will be, her womb irresistible. Toni feels dry, deficient of the sorrow and theatrics of sex. Her passion is in the undetected, her lust holds out for Spirit.

She hears Amalia in the toilet. "Thank you, God. Hey, Toni, I'm *bleeding*."

Toni, digging into her arm with fingernails, pressing red out of her famished, blue arm, says, "No, I am," and leaves to find Theodora.

Toni is biking back from seeing her therapist and swimming. The therapist was pleased by her weight gain; swimming, Toni was once more alone, the black crosses on the floor of the pool showing faces pale like beads, sad, oblong beads strung along the mournful, black cross she churned above.

Toni is thinking no matter what Theodora wears, it looks black. Her anguish, stubborn as blood, turns the fabric.

The white Cadillac is parked like a boat, like a damned yacht across the dirt in front of Anglada's. A week early. A week before they were supposed to pick her up. Shit. She drops the bike against the chipping green wall, shoves the velvet curtains and goes inside. Clarice is at the kitchen table, sipping something.

"Your father doesn't keep coffee, not even instant. God, I'm trying this herbal stuff, it's like gargling cologne. I don't know, Tones," she says, looking around. And Toni sees how shabby this place is with Clarice here, the magic shut off, concealed. Her mother looks worn, even in this shadowed kitchen, even with her sunglasses on, meaning she knows she looks terrible. She is wearing a white silk pantsuit with bunches of turquoise around her tanned, lined neck.

"This is such a berserk setup, how did you last this long? You should have let us know. God. We're in this gorgeous condo in Santa Fe. We thought we'd get up here a few days early, surprise you, rescue you I'd say at this point. We have opera tickets for tonight and want you to come with us."

"Can Dad come too?"

Clarice frowns, mashing her tea bag with the flat of a spoon.

"I don't know. We only have three tickets and I'm positive they're sold out. Maybe another time," she says with familiar cheerful deceit. She wouldn't be caught dead with Raymond.

"So, what do you do here? I haven't gotten one word from you. No postcard, no letter, *nada*."

"Ah, swim, bike around, stuff."

"Oh. Great. Sounds fun. Right." Clarice sighs.

"So where are the dads?"

"They walked down the road to buy beer, I guess. Well, Tones, how about showing me your room. Gee, do you have a room?"

They are sitting in the middle of the roller rink, on the dusty floor, drinking so much beer her mother is actually beginning to have fun, to laugh with Raymond enough so Toni can imagine the attraction at one time, maybe. Her stepfather is trying hard, in his madras sport coat and gold bracelet, not to make waves for anybody, his face more florid than usual. Toni excuses herself to go through the quiet garden with its intricate, white flowers, bridal lace, to knock at the door. After a little while, Theodora answers.

"My parents are here for me. I was afraid you'd be asleep."

"No, no. I laid down and couldn't sleep. So. Tell me how next time you visit, you'll be so fat, so big, I'll need somebody to introduce us."

"Yeah right. A real pig. Snarf." Toni makes a pig sound.

"Remember to eat for God, and if that doesn't work, then eat for me so I won't worry."

Theodora cups Toni's thin fingers around something bunchy, cool, in her hand. Kisses her.

Outside Anglada's, where Toni hears her parents, all three of them, laughing, practically choking on their own wit or whatever, she opens up her hand. Dulled black beads, the thin silvery Christ, caught like a tiny fish on Theodora's rosary. Taking her in. Feeding her. One hunger exchanged for another.

In the air-conditioned Cadillac, Toni persuades them to take the high mountain road to see the santuario. It's the most famous church in northern New Mexico, she says. Clarice sniffs, she has no interest in churches, but Toni's stepfather, not unkind, says, Let's stop, what can it hurt, Toni says it's something special.

But when they get to Chimayo, there are tour buses, the parking lot is full of cars, rows and rows of cars, a watery polish across their hoods. There is a gift shop Toni doesn't remember, selling holy water, medals, religious articles, souvenirs.

She's self-conscious beside this elegant woman who attracts lust, envy, beside her stepfather with his gold jewelry and white leather shoes. The church feels absent, the church is not there, although tourists crowd its shell, take pictures, set up picnics outside its walls. Toni wants the holy water but stops herself, avoiding her mother's ridicule. Already Clarice is stage-whispering, You brought the camera, did you bring the camera, her husband hissing, Yes, yes . . . Clarice yakking on, oh charming, so primitive, folk art is very collectible, all the while instructing her husband what pictures to take. Toni doesn't want them in the special rooms, but Clarice notices people going in there and wants to see.

Inside, the three of them watch an elderly Spanish woman dribbling dirt into a paper bag, most of the dirt falling over her shoes, she is so feeble, praying Our Father.

"Poor thing," Clarice whispers to Toni. "Superstition is so fascinating. This type of ignorance."

"I'm dying from these candles," her red-faced husband says. "There's absolutely no air. Can we go?"

"I'll be out in a minute," Toni answers.

Kneeling, famished, tongue lapping God's dryness. Feeding dirt into the tin she's taken from her purse, mouth working God, crossing herself with soured water down her meager face, all mixed with earth.

El Ojito del Muerto
(Eye of the Dead One)

Obedient to blithely imperious daughters wedging her into an orchid prom dress, the oldest tourniqueting a lace dresser scarf about her throat, the youngest hopping on the bed with Tinkerbell makeup, blotching frosted lavender above the eyes, fuchsia on and off the lips, bull's-eyes of rouge over the cheeks, the conclusive irony of a rhinestone tiara clamped on her middle-aged head, amusing her. Indulgent to children she adores, resigned to a life she had hoped to love.

With theatric pomp for so small a circumstance, they lead her, white half-slips on their heads, black polyester skirts belted against their chests, draping in stubby columns to the floor. Nuns. Freshly enrolled in Catholic school, her daughters compulsively act out ritual, impose doctrine. Tchaikovsky's *Swan Lake*, gargling and tinny, accompanies them from the Fisher-Price record player to the arched entry of an adobe living room, where Alan, her husband, and the young Hispanic man are remudding a corner fireplace.

Her youngest tugs her, trepid and embarrassed, off the top step, while the oldest makes trumpeting sounds.

"Hey, Dad. Check out Mom. We made her beautiful."

The young man turns to see. Their father crooks his head out of the fireplace, smiles, asks about lunch.

Orchid taffeta rustles under the baggy, knee-length gray sweatshirt as she serves lunch. She watches him dump half a jar of salsa on his hamburger, hears him say he'd like to take off work tomorrow and go hunting. Observes Alan, an ecologically hypersensitive man, in his favorite T-shirt, DON'T EAT ANYTHING WITH A FACE, being only hypocritically vegetarian, scarfing down two hamburgers.

Perched on the counter, she swings her feet, swishing the taffeta loud, on purpose.

"Gee, I'd like to go. What is it you're hunting?"

"Deer."

Alan scrapes his chair back.

"Well, you two go hunting, shoot up a storm, though I'm adamantly opposed to the decimation of wildlife, and I hope you don't come across anything but trees, rocks and roadkill, all that's left out there anyway."

Alan hikes up his pants, grins or grimaces, she can't tell most of the time, leaves the kitchen. From the living room, they hear him belch hugely before answering the phone, fielding yet another business call. Alan is a wildly successful tile manufacturer.

He brings his plate and her husband's to the sink, rinses them while looking at her, the frowzy dress, virulent makeup.

"Thank you. Lunch was excellent."

"You're quite welcome. I noticed you like salsa."

"Did you mean it about going hunting?"

"Yes. I really do want to go, but only if I don't have to kill anything. Have you heard of *Waiting for Godot*? It's this play where one of the characters, Vladimir, says, 'Habit is a great deadener.' Since my last birthday, I've been breaking habits. If I go, I'll just watch, I'll be a hunting voyeur."

"That's fine. I'll come for you tomorrow at four-thirty, so we can get to the mountains by first light. You have wool socks, gloves, long underwear?" He is scanning her body. "I have an extra pair of camouflage pants I got at the flea market, and an orange vest. I'll bring those for you."

"Do I bring the VCR? Just kidding. Can you imagine, home hunting videos?"

"No, that's okay, I'll bring everything."

She sets out the girls' lunch, then watches them awhile from the living-room window. They are kneeling inside the walled garden, beside an oval of fresh-dug dirt, profiles uptilted in morbid prayer. Her oldest intones from Alan's childhood Catholic missal, now an occult prop. Her youngest grips an unlit pink dinner candle. The pet cemetery has become heavily overrun in the month they have been here. One cat, a road victim. Two birds, cat victims. And four lunch bags of shriveling pet-shop mice, tied and swaying like homemade ornaments from the arthritic crab apple. She won't ask, doesn't want to know. Children assault animals with wild swings of adoration and neglect.

She watches out the same window, this time seeing his truck, headlights plowing like twin stars up the driveway lined with brittle, naked elms. Her husband and children are asleep at the farthest black end of the hallway.

She has trouble with the camouflage pants, has to come out of the bathroom; he kneels to unknot and retie strings that gather around the ankles. "Long underwear?" She nods, embarrassed. He stands up. He has to touch her hips to secure the canteen, the hunting knife in its leather sheath. They whisper.

"What?"

"I feel like a female guerrilla."

"What's this?"

"What's what? Oh. An altar. The girls made it." She hands him a stick of incense. "They like playing church. Weddings with no groom. Funerals. Mostly funerals."

They walk out to the truck; purple-black, freckled with white mud, punched in numerous places. Red bandannas with black electrical tape bandage the broken taillights. In the truck bed are two chunks of cedar, a rotted tire, length of rope, plastic water jug, tricycle wheel and four or five beer cans. She knows this even in darkness. Once when he had left his truck on their property to go fishing with friends, Alan had discovered her, sitting, just sitting in it. She'd made a lame excuse about getting out of the heat, which Alan distractedly, good-naturedly (naive for all his intelligence), accepted.

She gets in on his side, the other door broken, sidles under the steering wheel. The seat's caved in, stuffed with blankets and towels. Clumsy in her hunting regalia, she knocks the glove box, so the front piece drops, hangs by a hinge. Receipts, cards, feathers, a box of bullets — she catches some in her hands, scoops the rest from the floor, apologizing.

Handing her the rifle, he gets in, slams the door. The truck clanks, rattles like a junk drawer, the heater abrades her face with silty, hot air, the gun anchored across her lap. A Winchester 243, an elk etched into the oak butt, she traces it with her thumb. In the green and violet light off the dash, she watches him stick the incense where black vinyl has peeled down to foam.

Heading into the mountains, in his truck, with its Clearasil tinted interior, broken speedometer, needle gyrating (Mach 10, we're at Mach 10, he says) . . . the highway a black current beneath the torn gear boot, candy wrappers, work gloves, rolls of electrical tape, toilet paper, sun-rotted parrot feathers fanning out of the visor, catprints arrowing up the windshield, a yellow apple mushing against the windshield, binoculars, bullets, a Chinese noodle mix, the whole inside stinking of soured sponge, overheated plastic and dead, crumbling Styrofoam. He is telling a joke about two drunk mice and Elvis Presley.

"Coffee?" She lofts the thermos. "We can share from the cup-thingy on top."

"Sure." He navigates a dirt road sculpted with potholes and washboard gullies, saying he graded this road for the Forest Service two years before. Compressed against the roadsides are gothic, violet spires of ponderosa, streaks of white aspen. He is looking at her.

"What are you thinking?"

"How I was a member of the Canadian and American Wolf Defenders League, the Wild Horse and Burro Association, how I had Save the Whale, what else, oh, Save the Dolphin stickers on my old station wagon in Illinois. I'm an environmentalist, so I'm feeling guilty. I'm also a conflicted vegetarian."

"Conflicted?"

"My mind rejects meat but my stomach won't."

"Well, we're not out here shooting animals for the sick thrill of it. My family's always hunted for survival, we use every part of the deer, the elk."

"You're saying you're not a sport hunter?"

"You bet. I'm not one of those guys who flies in not knowing wildlife from his own ass."

"I love deer. Actually I love armadillos. I was going to buy an armadillo, until somebody said they give you leprosy. Can you believe it?"

He hits a deep gully and they both fly off the seat, her head grazes the ceiling and she slops coffee all over.

"Oops. Your pants, sorry. Camouflage works. They should make children's clothes of this stuff."

He laughs. They've reached the mountaintop, fishtailing across a wide, grassy clearing. Behind a low, dark hump of mountains, light flows like spilt water, blurring perfect seams of fuchsia, tangerine, violet. He stops the truck, and they sit together in an odd, detective-type silence.

"Look. There they are."

Gracefully he draws the rifle off her lap, rolls the window, pushes the barrel out, sighting. She doesn't see a thing, then four deer swiftly bearing down on the truck, passing in an elegant, dreamy arc. He draws the rifle in.

"Does. Flushed out from those woods over there."

"Do people shoot does?"

"Last year, one guy shot one from his truck, split her straight up the ass, got out, dragged her to the side of the road, took off. Idiot. Yeah, it happens."

The sun is on the mountain, the grass, the barbed fences steadily brightening.

"What do we do now?"

"Keep looking. Plus I'll teach you to shoot so you can go after your first deer."

"God, I really don't think I can do that." Yet she feels shamed by a sudden, eerie wish to do what he accepts as natural.

The truck grinds, crawls. Once in a while, they pass hunters in other trucks and everyone waves, solemn, oathlike. She feels bored, having imagined hunting as stalking through woods or crouching behind individual trees, not cruising in a truck, staring out dirt-crazed windows into greenish black pools of trees and hazy stubble of oak, visually straining after a white flash of deer tail.

"Do they know? The deer?"

"That we're looking for them? You bet. They'll stash under rock ledges, or go with the elk after elk season's over."

"All I know is so far we've seen four does and entire herds of neutered beer cans."

They start counting cans. By the time they get to a hundred on both sides of the road, they're down to the highway, the sun on the center stripe, the exact gold of fallen cottonwood leaves. He heads the truck up another forest service road, sunlight soaking the air, varnishing the sea blue pines, hitting into flat red earth, picked with white stone. Out her opened window, the air is thin and smells of turpentine. He stops, reads aloud a historic marker: 1540, Coronado's scouts, 1598, colonists used this road to settle New Spain. El Camino Real. Oldest road in the United States of America.

The dirt road, thin as a hall, this oldest road, is piled and gouged with boulders. The truck shrieks up an increasingly precarious angle of ruts and clefts. Striking a partly submerged rock, it bucks, lists hideously to her side, stops. He yanks the brake, gets out, disappears by the tire on her side. She hears his voice.

"You're not gonna believe . . ."

"The tire came off . . ." She's joking.

His face comes up, a puppet in the stage of her window.

"Correct. We're thrown."

They are now stuck on the oldest road in the United States of America. She helps as he calls for rocks to prop up the wrenched tire, directs him as he coasts the truck backward, downhill, swerving into a flat, weedy area, sits beside his camouflaged legs thrust from under the truck, leather boots sprawling up, hands him pliers, baling wire he happened to have. It's the steering rod mechanism, he's seen one of his uncles fix the same thing on his truck with wire and pliers.

"Did you know Hispanics buy parts cheap and can fix anything?" His voice muscles, cheerful, from under the truck.

"Nope. I didn't know that."

"Cheap parts because we don't have any money. Fix anything since we're smart. There. That should get us back to town."

Famished, cheerful, they eat everything in his pack. He army-knifes an orange in a zigzag design . . . there, a flower, presenting one pretty half to her. Lays Cheez-Its on the rough mountain grass, one corner against another, a flat formation of cracker butterflies. He shows her how to hold the Winchester, sight down the scope, pull back the trigger, shows her how to aim on an animal. A deer. And later, when he lies back to rest in the long mountain grass, she lies near him, asleep for several hours, like a child.

In the stifling truck, bumping cautiously, they pass a prim geometry of bicyclists in glistening black shorts, white helmets, colored flags snapping precisely. Her husband, Alan, is a bicycle racer. Competitive, ardent. She used to go to races with him, thinking at first how handsome he looked, later, how morose with competitive lust. Often he won. In Chicago, the Museum of Science and Industry has a gigantic human heart you can walk into pressing buttons to hear the heart talk, explain itself. Her daughters used to pull her in and out of that heart, over and over. Right now, she remembers this.

She spots it first, standing on the highway's edge, in the restrained, verdigris light of early evening, so utterly still as to make her think it is false.

"Oh God."

He swerves the truck onto the gravel shoulder. "Okay. Put your gun out the window, sight the way I showed you, and pull the trigger."

"I can't."

"Do it. Just the way I showed you."

She sights, seeing it in the little scope, a wire-thin cross over the concealed heart.

She misses, hits the neck. The deer stumbles, regains itself, weakly runs.

"Go after it. I'll find you. Go. Take the gun. You may have to shoot again, the way I showed you."

Comes upon it in a sparse grass clearing, collapsed, doesn't understand whether to shoot or not. Dropping to her knees beside its head, she sees its antlers, white-tipped candelabra, the gorgeous eye fearful, her face miniaturized in its glazing surface. The breathing sounds hoarse, choppy, blood raveling from the earth side of the mouth. Her own breathing alters, suffers. She feels coarse, reverent. As a child, she'd rehearsed small, sweet cruelties on pets, now her daughters tenderly bully weaker creatures. She is exultant, stricken.

Standing above them, unsheathing his knife, he stoops to yank the deer so its exquisite head and sorrel neck slant down-hill, slices the throat. Blood forming uneven collars around rocks, thickening, collecting, cherry red, stinking. Its eye open, hind legs kicking, still fleeing.

He sits on his boot heels, wipes the blade edge along grass.

"Now we wait for all the blood to drain. Want something to drink?"

She shakes her head.

"You all right?" Reaches over, sets a blood hand on her shoulder. "You're doing good. You feel sick? Quite a few people get sick at first, it's nothing to be embarrassed about. Wait here, I'm going to the truck to get a soda."

Seated in the company of death, blood thinning into arterial, still-exuberant rivers. She's been reading a book about medieval Spanish nuns, their journals, poetry. Reading about nuns chronically, tyrannically bled to take out the Devil's afflictions. Affliction malefic in the blood.

Drinks his Coke, takes his knife, cuts its testicles.

"You can turn these inside out to cover gearshift knobs. People do that," he tells her. Hacks off what he calls stinkers from the ankles, removing anything that taints the meat. His knife slides from the anus to the stomach, left whole with its fermenting grasses, gutting to the throat. Steam climbs out from the deer, a stink from gases caught between ribs and intestines. All the deer's arcane interior is dumped out for scavenger birds, the deer's dark, complex interior broken apart into humid junk.

He halves the heart, and she pours water from the red and white plastic jug, laving the heart like a great, dark, broken bowl. The rinsed halves slide off his hand into a plastic bag. Disk of flat, greenish liver, wine-colored kidneys, put with the heart, *asaduras*, he says. Delicious. His arms are brilliant red past the elbow. She floods water into the exposed cavity of deer, polishing the hollow of it.

Purpose graces his body, the shape of lowered head, the long hair, its curls like obsidian, with its bits of blue and red, the concentrated curve of spine, the deer's wildness perished and gone into him. Inordinate blood, red haze on the evening, the gray, languorous guts, the smell. She imagines, like him, planting her arms in the deer, in its pearled wreathing of ribs, her arms would be like his then, Chinese red, thick smelling, and purged of affliction.

He ropes the antlers and front feet together, and they drag the deer up through shrub to the road. Two hunters come by, help lift it into the truck bed. They speak Spanish, and do not look at her, which she thinks is politeness, respect or hostility.

When he cleans her arms with a strip of torn shirt, both of them look at her arms smeared with blood. She thinks she has never seen her arms before, not really, their freckled pinkness, narrow wrists, work-thickened knuckles. Her hands look so much older than her arms, they embarrass her. She looks instead into his face, his eyes focus on her nails, wiping tendrils of deer's blood from the oval beds of her fingernails.

In the garage behind the house where he lives with his grandmother, aunt and cousins, he uses rope to suspend the deer from a beam, begins to slice the hide, peel back the cape, exposing the meat. Like taking off tights, she thinks weirdly, obliquely, sitting on an old oil drum in one corner of the garage, eerily lit, like a bar, with one small ceiling bulb. A cousin comes out from the house to help, she hears this cousin, in Spanish say *amor,* nod toward her. She hears him on the other side of the deer laughing, saying no. She hears her husband's name.

She is wondering how to interpret this place she has so idealistically moved to, the hacienda she and Alan will restore, the horses they will buy, the tiled pool they will build in the courtyard, embellished with huge clay pots of trailing red geranium. Her Mexican coffee table with its precise arrangement of books on the Southwest, on southwestern interior design, on southwestern landscaping, on New Mexican history. She just purchased another expensive book on Spanish door and window designs. And yesterday, she'd purchased two ristras of lacquered chilies to hang on either side of the massive front door. And now, sitting on this oil drum in a small, cluttered garage, facing the stucco house he has grown up in, old cars thrown and dismembered around the dirt yard, the clothesline, with jeans, T-shirts, dishcloths neatly pinned. The deer hanging between the two young men, in their worn shirts and jeans, expertly dividing the animal from itself.

Outside the house, he rubs his arms under the hose, chipping the dry blood, the water gray, wintry.

"Would you like to have supper with us? My aunt will want to cook the lomo, the part I told you about that runs along the spine? She uses butter and a little brandy, it's excellent."

"I should call home." She had been going to say call my husband.

"Oh, there's no phone. We can go to my neighbor's and call."

"Well, no. I suppose I'd better get home."

"You sure? Let me wrap some meat for you to take home to your family."

She cannot imagine her children, the little nuns, with hunks of deermeat in their roseate mouths.

She waits in his kitchen, near the back door, while he cuts the meat near the sink. The house is overly warm and smells of pine cleaning products. The TV is on in a room off the kitchen, and she hears the same news announcer she'd listened to in her kitchen in Illinois. A cedar crucifix hangs above the clean, white sink. He wraps the foil, his hands careful. She notices how he attends to what is before him.

"There. *Gracias a Dios.*" He grins sweetly. "We always thank God when we receive a deer for food."

Her heart, blocking her whole chest, keeps her from saying anything brittle or amusing. Back in his truck, they bump out the little, rutted dirt driveway, sitting close because of the hunting equipment on her side.

"So. Did you enjoy your day?"

"Oh yes. Very much." Dull, so stupid. She who is known for wit in crisis, has gone aphasic. She cannot breathe beside this man she scarcely knows.

"Do you mind if I hold your hand awhile?" He says this, his hand already on hers.

They drive to her house, down the long elm-lined driveway. The house, sprawling and huge, is dark.

She feels how close behind her he stands as she twists the key until the front door opens. She's self-conscious about the ornamental ristras beside the door, after seeing the homemade one in his kitchen, unlacquered, used for cooking.

She reads Alan's note, left on the kitchen table, while he opens the refrigerator, puts in the deermeat.

"Oh. They've gone down to Albuquerque to see one of Alan's bicycle friends. He says he'll call in the morning — "

He hadn't even signed the note to her.

The girls left drawings; the oldest colored her in the orchid prom dress, the youngest drew two heart heads, lopsided hearts with human features and stick bodies.

Perhaps there are times when one's fate is predestined by those acts which came before, leading, maplike, to the present. During the long and irreversible span of devastation and betrayal to come, during the time her face became like the empty eye of the deer, she would ask over and over how she might have resisted, might have gone some uncomplicated, purer way.

And in those moments it took to lightly throw her upon the bed, guard, then guardian, purchasing her with beautiful eyes, with hands earlier gone inside the deer now opening her legs, hands now inside her, looking in a hard, bold, natural way no one had ever before looked upon her flesh, hands, body, eyes, voice, in those moments her face surrendered its careful artifice, its years of artifice and taught pose, her face the deer she had killed, its spirit gone into his. So carefully placed as a vase upon the becalmed and lonely surface of her perfect life, so lonely, so careful, in her own life, doll in wife-clothes, doll in mother-clothes, doll in an orchid dress, doll in camouflage, now so humbly naked, herself in a white bathtub in the ivory bathroom, an ivory candle in its dull brass stick on the watery ledge of the tub, his thick legs wedged against hers, his hands smoothing her back with ovals of soapy washcloth. No one since her mother had washed her back so tenderly, so gravely.

Head down, neck vulnerable, she mentions the beauty of the deer, the finality of its death. The only death, until now, she had ever caused.

"But death is necessary for new life. *La muerte es necesario para la vida nueva,*" he said softly, rinsing her back with cupped hands, candlelight gilding her breasts and stomach, pulling her against him, showing how he cut and quartered the exquisite deer, his hands, callused and skillful, pushing her forward, her spine arching, slitting tender areas along the spine, cutting with imaginary blade her cleansed, white skin.

She tries defending herself, the safe life she has built, but her humor is weak, lost in dangerous context, deeper feeling.

"So are you done with killing the deer and me as well?"

By answer, lifting the water-heavy hair, dropping it along one shoulder, moving his lips down the damp, surrendered neck, giving the ungovernable authority of love, the godlike affliction of desire.

Uriel

With what brute artlessness did you instruct Uriel to feed himself — so he would more graciously starve? With what virulent innocence did you bathe him, in a climate where dust falls in excruciating burial, the wind an exhumation, the burial process unceasing, the dirt fine as cinnamon?

With what crucial purity did you stuff virgin hope into the heart of a child abandoned?

Uriel, How You Come to Meet Him

His mother serves a broken-handled cup of coffee, a tortilla pasted with rancid butter. In schoolroom Spanish, you introduce yourself, the American teacher come to Rivas to help her oldest son and others in the barrios. You swallow, nauseous on soured fat, not confessing your desertion from the elegant palace in Managua, where you had been assigned five children with cerebral palsy, children of the rich. You only ask to meet her son.

Uriel. Fire of God. Regent of the Sun, angel of the presence, archangel of salvation, heavenly interpreter of Ezra's visions, presider over repentance, prince of lights.

Spiritual idealism cannot spare you Uriel, a shell-like whorl on its naked side, in a crib of broken slats, facing a wall apparently blank, which you will come to believe has seraphim collecting beneath its mortared surface, the tips of wings striking blank plaster. Except for a rank gilding of urine, he is naked, oppressed by teeming air and an unendurable blankness. His mother speaks. It is impossible to feed him, to dress him, to do anything with him, he is too old, seventeen years old and too heavy for her, too much for her, for anyone in the house. His mother's face is sterile with misfortune; a gold twig of crucifix sticks to the cleft in her blouse as she nests her newest baby high on the knob of her shoulder.

Your first night in the sorrow that is Uriel's house, you lie beneath an unglassed window, the moon tilted in its square, a sallow marble on navy tile. Your red American bicycle glitters against a wall crumbling from mortar shells and bullet holes. Over the worst spot, you've taped a poster of a ballerina. Her milky back is to the world, her leg plunged out like a wand, arm hooped, severe. Renounce, the leg says. Renounce whatever is evil with time.

Through humid sleep, you hear the reedy squeal of a pig. Every morning, near dawn, a pig is slaughtered for market beneath your little window. By such little deaths, in this fashion, you are wakened.

Saint Teresa Singing

The more severe the suffering, the more palpable will be God. Does a shadow pass over your square places of dirt and cardboard and disease? It is Teresa, shading you from Pagan Sun. Embrace suffering as a swift route to the Beloved.

Somoza's troops laid siege here ten years ago. Many of you entered my church, bolting three metal doors against the enemy. The old people, the children and their mothers knelt down. A donkey, bloated in unnatural death, a gray and split-ting mango, lay across the steps of my church until the siege ended.

These soldiers, contras, after eating their own gunpowder to give them courage, after kissing the crucifixes around their necks, exploded the stained glass with mortars and rockets and guns. Bullets ricocheted inside the cool air of the church, and small birds of resplendent glass, banana and mango, blood and indigo, blew like blessed hail.

The North American woman who lives across the street seats herself before the glass shrine of Jesus of the Passion. She contemplates the three bullet holes in the head of Jesus of the Passion. Jesus, associated with tributaries of blood, has wounds bloodless and small. There are many huge saints in glass shrines in my church, elongated vases enclosing their fragrant, cool bloom. After ten years, the walls crumble, nothing has been repaired. Brilliant pennants of birds stream in, perch on the pews, along the altars, no one pays attention. There is blood in the choir loft, blood of someone, in dry, maroon patterns. Teresa sees how details of the revolution interest this woman. Your village is a history book, a page of political science, a chapter, a paragraph, she lives and breathes air still faintly damaged, tinged with smoke, scented with blood of pigs out-side her window, blood of pigs to stimulate her imaginings.

After prayer, she rides her cherry red bicycle dimmed by perpetual dust into the poorest of your slums, into streets where houses are collapsing cardboard pieces, where it is not uncommon to steer around another body in the streets, drunk or dead, who knows. She stops to photograph the body, face up in the filthy street, a proof no one will accept. She enters your impossibly hot, airless dwellings, seeking visibly damaged children, bringing food, sometimes clothing, rarely medicine as medicine does not exist here. She cradles babies as they fail and die in her own yellowing arms, sets her compassionate heart over wounds the length and breadth of nations. It seems to her beauty escapes to higher and higher elevations, to birds in the verdant tops of mango, coffee, banana trees.

In Rivas, it is said there are more bars than people. She meets him in these bars, the American lawyer who has spent many years in Nicaragua, Guatemala, Honduras. Her desire is not for him as for the revolution, its details, she wishes she had been here ten years before. Yet she transfers desire onto him in muddied, inarticulate, heartbreaking gestures.

The Lawyer

Arguing, her sweat disagreeable, her voice brassed and slurry. Am I doing Good, am I doing Harm? This obsesses her, an egocentric question. She feels like a strand of rain in the desert, dry before it hits the ground. I tell her she is arrogant to assign herself such a diminished place, to assume she knows the effects of her acts. Much of what we do vibrates in our absence. People here tolerate me because I will fight in courtrooms and streets for them. They do not love me because love must be reciprocal, and I am past that. I try to want this earnest, troubled woman, but I find fault: her bicycle, her hair dryer, her ballet poster, her religion — another twelve-week Lady Bountiful. When she breaks, I reassure but do not fool her. She says she is sick, her skin looks flayed with sweat. Am I doing Good, am I doing Harm?

Uriel in Water

At dawn the pig's throat is split, and you think, what if it was the same animal again and again, redeemed by sacrifice, not market?

You enter Uriel's room naked, the birds are mute, the blackened air smells of tropical chewing gum, of Uriel's grayed sweat and rich stink. You make out only the round water slicks of his eyes, the slim planks of teeth as he smiles up from the crib. His smile, very beautiful, is reserved for you; over this you harbor seductive vanity. You haul Uriel from his crib, down the hall to a small bathroom, your feverish arms clipped under arms that have embraced nothing in seventeen years. The shower has only cold water, yet in Rivas this is undisputed wealth, any water at all.

Who is not restored, carried into hope, by the presence of a clean-smelling child? You scrub Uriel's flesh, darkened in waste, with a washcloth and brick of soap. His body's tuneless palsy reminds you of a fish exiled from water, convulsed in a hostile environment. In a cold smear of water, you are both exonerated, the cries from his throat and leaping mouth distinct with joy. His eyes stay on yours, always, fixed in contrast to the body, which roils and bops with such dissonance. You dry and dust him with powder, pin on a cloth diaper, seesaw over his head your Dick Tracy T-shirt, asking yourself about his sexuality at seventeen. Uriel's retardation is so fathomless, his body in such anarchy, you begin doing what you have always done with inanimate objects, imposing fantasies, qualities, thoughts, desires, projecting a kind of anthropomorphism on him. You imbue this boy with metaphysical significance, with original Fear.

His mother stands in faraway, polite relationship. Her acceptance of you is never to be mistaken for welcome, compressed by an essential caution too terrible to express, a woman who lost one infant when a mortar fragment slammed between its cheekbone and eye, another to malaria because there was no medicine; that, she insists, was the only reason. Medicine, education, food, these have become extinct in Rivas. There is enough suffering here to collapse a universe, yet the world goes daily on and much that is beautiful here seems to be out of reach, elevated, sky high. The primary, Crayola-hued birds, the feast-day pinks, scarlets and citrines of blossoms in trees, the painted saints in glass havens, soaring sideways and serene.

Saint Teresa Singing

The whole village, as one dark, squinted Eye, sees how she secures him with an elastic cord before jumping the wheelchair back down two broken steps. Along the dust- and sun-drowned streets, wheelchair spokes flash like narrow, starving trout.

Such sincere, impossible effort, watering a dead stick, proclaiming it will be a tree, faith surpassing insanity, the way she stops every little while because he has slumped so far the tips of his feet clumsily farrow dirt, and she must stop to haul him upright, refasten the elastic again and again, impossible numbers of times. What slapstick, what sweethearts, laterally buffeting your wretched hearts.

Three scalding and dirty blocks to the mercado, where she arranges fruit, vegetables and pink sweets on his dishlike lap. She pays too much, willingly. Then she rolls Uriel in a happy gluttonous rush, bumps him up the several steps and inside the café, pushes him up to one of the five plain tables. The radio, always on, plays one of the two AM stations in Rivas. She orders coffee for herself, a dish of ice cream for Uriel.

Here the Eye averts, embarrassed, as she begins feeding him with the flat gray spoon ice cream for which he is crazy, acts completely crazy. He has never tasted ice cream, he has never eaten without spitting everywhere. He shouts and spits and drools milky spit, a process of anger and mess. Over weeks, this woman turns canny, making him wait between mouthfuls, refusing the next spoonful if he spits or tantrums, gently clamping his head with her arm so he can better control the muscles of his mouth and jaw and throat, his eyes turning, willful, on her. In between bites, digging up a bit of ice cream, holding his head, prodding the spoon inside the wet, unpredictable twist of his mouth, she drinks her coffee. The two elderly sisters stare, their restaurant deserted except for this and the radio playing. She turns and grins at them. Hey! He loves your good ice cream! Yes! *Cómo le gusta tu bueno ice crema!*

So resolute, so cheerful, with such stubborn will teaching the impossible, feeding a crazy boy, wasting sweets on a crazy boy. The radio, stubborn also, puts out a miracle of fast sound in the slow, agonizing torpor, the ice cream a moony pool at the bottom of the small, pink dish. She mops his face with her spit, the sweet ordeal over.

Sometimes, this woman goes on, pushing Uriel toward the west, outside the village to a mango plantation. She lifts him out of the wheelchair onto someplace soft and begins to talk, speaking in English as, with Uriel, it doesn't matter. It is so hard here, she tells him, so terrible here, there is no end to the suffering. Sometimes she talks about the lawyer, how he is cold justice lacking heart for her or for anyone. She talks on and on in the depths of the mango plantation, her words spreading into green monotony. And your rapacious Eye, missing nothing, pursues her down dirt paths into cardboard and tin shacks, into my martyred church, or into the stifling bars, you mothers in your one whisper, Teresa hears how you discuss with pity and with pity, her.

Ballet for Uriel

You move in darkness before the lawyer, who tells you life is not the simple tension of good and evil you live by. Ballet. Clumsily pure. What good you do for another is evil for someone else. You spin before this political man, nauseous. We live off death until one day we join the great organism of Death. It is all about feast, he says. Feast? You do splits, telling him about the pigs butchered under your window. He falls back, declaring he would love waking to that. Drunk, very drunk, drunk little skunks, and you, tumbling around on a bluff over-looking the lake. Lake Nicaragua is this great body of water that makes you need to pee, so you do. Sex is probably more on your mind than his, a vaguely humiliating issue. He has a puffy belly, mean-colored hair, his ego is colossal, his ego is an empty barn, there is nothing lovely about him, or is it his con-tempt for your ideals, which is, perhaps, envy distorted, that makes him perversely attractive?

Are you a virgin? Tell me. How long have you been a virgin?

He is convinced you are a virgin. Reply with a question.

Do you have a girlfriend?

Two. I have at least two. One in Managua, another in Guatemala.

Do they know each other?

Of course not. They are both pretty and remarkably dumb.

Pretty and dumb?

Yes. Both pretty, both dumb. Neither one is complicated or tiresome. Neither one is political or religious. That's refreshing.

That's racist, sexist, judgmental.

Racist, sexist, judgmental. He mocks you. And how long will you last here? For some reason, his arm gestures toward the lake, the wrong direction. He starts in on you, opens up on you, this flaw, that flaw, this ideal, that ideal, a litany of weak-ness until, edging sideways, downhill toward town, you ignore his silly authority.

In foul, unlit streets men approach, their bodies half-dead, soft flies you swat away with your empty bottle. They fall back, timid. Such predictable incidents, such easy defeat. Your little triumph, as you go inside Uriel's house, disproportionate, to hide an embellishing weight of sorrow.

You stand over him a long time, hearing wings with a hollow clap, like his peed-on sheets shaken hard under the blank plaster, above the blond crib. You strain to hear unearthly, merciful voices.

A fake pig-snort under your window. The lawyer's burly head rises like a cynical moon in the window. He climbs in and passes out next to you, snoring like hell's weather, his hands gripping your waist in some desperate companionable impotence. You would wish to place every child in Rivas, untouched and pure, inside a glass shrine in the cathedral of Saint Teresa.

Uriel smiles at you in the bathroom. He has no way to understand you are leaving him. Shrined inside water, you kiss his lips, his cheeks, his chin, his hair, his neck, his shoulders, his chest, then stomach, thighs, groin, knees, calves, the arches of each foot. Flesh heals, and you understand you will never act this perfectly again. With this degree or sublimity of love.

In the Final Presence of Saint Teresa

I know you, each one. I am the sourness within your houses, I am concealed in walls, cries, kisses, in the eyes of the elderly sisters who say the boy's progress is a miracle, the boy, they tell her, adores you, he would die for you, it is a miracle you have come.

Suffering is the swiftest route to the Beloved.

On the night before the North American will abandon him, I am present as they lie naked on her bed, Uriel graced by sleep as he can never be otherwise. I tell you he will feed off her absence, he will live on her absence, one night he will die of this absence.

In a dark cheat of sleep, their incorrupt, guileless hunger lifts Saint Teresa in minor elevation above the dancer's arching spine, split radiant, into wings.

On Faith Alone

For days, Ted Padilla had me bicycling past the dead Indian, bicycling past a blanket stubbed like a wet cheroot in dirty ditchweed — how did I know what was or wasn't vital, being new to town? Soon after, he had me spading into mouse-colored soil behind the warehouse, delving for Anasazi artifacts until I realized this, like the bogus Indian, was another instance of Ted's rural wit. So when I informed him someone was making a home inside one of his moving crates, Ted disbelieved, until I marched him to the south side of the warehouse and pried back a loosened panel of crate.

"Air conditioning's broken, ha, ha."

"No, this is pathetic. Do you know who this is?"

"Nope." Actually, I had snuck twice inside the crate, stepping over a snail's hump of sleeping bag, squeezing the half loaf of Rainbo white, sniffing at the jar of peanut butter and snapping with my thumb until it quivered, a pocketknife impaled in one plywood wall. I'd even watered the philodendron, its waxen-hearted leaves draining from a canary yellow pot. I had noted female detritus. Earrings. A skinny-waisted, blue pearled comb.

Solicitous of my soul, Ted brings me to a revival on the east side of town. Inside a thick hide of tent, its umber flanks hollowed, tall fans lash air over families in metal row chairs the drab color of bleached chocolate. We are here to witness Eulogia Vigil weep oil from her two palms. Eulogia — Ted's cousin and a former bagger at the local supermarket, fired for getting everybody's groceries greasy, is today a rhinestone of faith on the small-town circuit, a miracle jewel wedged between the Kiddie Karnival and Men in Motion, an itinerant male striptease. According to Ted, the town is split between who has faith and who doesn't in the holy authority of Eulogia's palms. I was raised in a household emptied of deities, so out of an old deprivation rather than any mature conviction, I believe, ever so blithely, in Eulogia's palms.

In the seat directly before me, a boy neatly vomits as his parents, along with other grown-ups, wave uplifted arms and whisper a sibilant, mock-Hebrew known as "tongues." Even Ted, my prospective husband, the manager of a moving and storage company, is doing this. I raise my own arms, trailing them, and discover a vibrant band of energy, a red-colored emotional current two feet overhead.

Dramatic organ music brings Eulogia to the platform, shrink-wrapped in black polyester, her hair inflated into a black, glossy bubble. Her lips are brutally red. Should I keep one eye on those dramatic, tubular sleeves, a winter outfit in all this heat, might she not have cruets of salad oil stuck up each one? But miracles mocked make poor miracles, so at the tiny, mordant vision of her, each of us, infected by excess carbon dioxide, falls theologically limp. The especially raptured, led forward, buckle beneath Eulogia's oily thump to their foreheads, felled to the dirt by faith.

I glance sideways at Ted, normally a nice-looking Hispanic man, and see the whites of his eyeballs. Both my arms are lifeless from being upraised, my armpits rankle. You can tell who's gone up by the shiny brooches on their foreheads. I am set to go, a strip of air widening between my seat and me, when one of the men framing Eulogia, Brother Shiloh, his pumpkin-colored hair gelled into a trough, starts shouting Eulogia has enemies in her hometown, those who wish her harm, and yes, oh yes, there is one young woman among them tonight, an unprincipled young woman who does not believe, and if she does not come humbly forward, will die or cause another to die in thirty days due to some sort of mechanical accident. Woeful scythe, Brother Shiloh hunches over the microphone. Eulogia embosses shining planets on one brow after another. No young woman steps forward. Her salvation time expires. The organ whumps histrionically. I sit down, terrified.

"Did you like it?"

Ted, forehead glossy in the street light, idles his brand-new, company truck in front of my rented house. He will not come inside. Sex can wait, he likes to think, until after marriage. I don't mind. After a reckless past, I gravitate to carefulness, rules, method. To someone like Ted Padilla.

"I don't think it's fair to threaten people. What if he meant me? If he meant me, you or I might both be dead before our wedding."

The thought inspires Ted to vault his own rule and kiss me. I kiss back, and this is correct, the next morning we will wake up, in my bed, in my rented house, released from all formal constraints of purity.

Ted has me focusing his hunting binoculars, spying on the crate, waiting for somebody to come in or go out. He has set bait, a bright sack of potato chips, a missile-shaped liter of Mountain Dew and a note:

> Please come to the office. We won't hurt you. You are not in danger. We want to help. God loves you. Ted Padilla, Manager.

When a skimpy figure in camouflage pants and a black sleeveless T-shirt creeps backwards out of the crate with the liter of Mountain Dew, I sling the binoculars to Ted, who instantly identifies his cousin.

"It's Chrissie."

"Who?"

"My cousin, Chrissie. He's supposed to be in jail — well, juvenile home in Springer."

"No. What for?"

"Bet he's looking for Vernice."

"Who's that?"

"She had his baby a couple of weeks ago. But she's moved to Chacón."

Ted steps outside, yells to his cousin and minutes later, the three of us set out for Holman to deliver a swing set and a rototiller, and to figure out what to do. Holman is a spotty mountain village, pop. 80, where four years ago, the face of

Jesus surfaced, a sienna stain on an outside wall of the Catholic church. Pilgrims showed up by the thousands, mostly at night, when the face was said to be plainly burdened and sorrowful. Ted had taken his grandmother twice, his aunt once. All three times, the face looked upon him with irrefutable command. Ted quit drinking, quit dope, labored his way out of destructive habits. When I met Ted, he had evolved into an evangelist of ambition, responsibility and unimpugned credit. Sometimes, I am embarrassed by how hard he works to do everything right. Still, I take refuge in his earnestness, which, like books and other printed instructions, distracts and consoles me.

The Pak Van, used for small moving jobs, is an ivory-colored, cube-shaped truck manufactured by the prison industry. I sit, a bit rocky, in the pink lawn chair Ted jammed between himself and Chrissie, who's slunkered on the passenger side, a black bandanna knotted around his black hair, coarse, dragging past his shoulders, the exact rubber tire color of his T-shirt. Chrissie's profile, arrogant and vulpine, shows the doomed cunning of a nearly extinct animal. One of his front teeth is bashed out, and in hard angles of light, I see his skin like tinwork, faintly pocked. Worried he has a gun in one of the large hip pockets of his camouflage pants, I try staring at landscape instead of the conspicuous lump on the half of his body nearest me. The arid, wavy hillsides, I decide, look like palomino hide studded with piñon saddle sores. When Chrissie draws a bottle of vodka, not a gun, from his pocket, Ted and I, primly bonded, decline.

In front of a tin-roofed adobe church, four emaciated horses, hobbled to stakes, crop ashen weeds. Ted parks the van beside one horse, entangled up to its muzzle in a chokecherry hedge, and escorts me to the now featureless west wall of the church. Chrissie, with his bottle, has crawled back over the seats to rock abjectly in the candy-striped swing set. On our way back from the church wall, I stop to unfasten the horse from the hedge. Ted tries yanking me away.

"No. You're likely to get shot out here messing with people's animals."

"Shot in a churchyard?"

"Out here, you never know. You mess in other people's business, you can get killed."

I persist, the closest we come to any ethical argument.

The three of us unload the rototiller, the swing set, and leave Holman. In the Pak Van, after Ted tells Chrissie Vernice has moved with the baby to her father's place in Chacón, he lectures his cousin . . . take responsibility for what you've done, pay the consequence, then start over, like I did. Chrissie reacts with boozy geniality to the news that Ted will be driving him back to the juvenile home right after he finishes a moving job in Las Cruces.

The following morning, on my reception desk, I find a florist's bouquet and in the ashtray, the still-shiny keys to Ted's truck. Both gifts make me chary. I am having last-minute qualms about being settled, much less married, partly due to a book I am reading on self-esteem. I have what the author calls "happiness anxiety," a compulsion to subvert anything good into crisis. Ted knows nothing of this. All he knows is my soul appears salvageable, and for all my college education, I prove remarkably easy to fool.

Made anxious, I go out and tack a note to the crate, emboldened by the mercy of my motive. I don't wait long — by late afternoon, I am in Ted's truck, driving Chrissie out to Chacón.

As the truck idles on one side of a wire fence, cowboy boots sticking heel-up on all the posts, pointing at an aquamarine trailer anchored in peaks and swells of reddish mud, Chrissie and I have our first conversation since leaving the warehouse.

"I forgot a present."

"Present?"

I sound this dumb because I have never suffered so little effect on anyone. I'm not used to it.

"The baby. I didn't bring anything." Chrissie pouts, forlorn, an infant himself.

"Here." I shove my purse across the seat. "I bought them for Ted, but they'll make a great baby gift."

He digs around, finds the package, starts reading.

"Starlights. Glow in the Dark Stars. One Hundred and Forty Self-Adhesive Stars, Moons, Planets, Comets, and Quasars."

"You stick them on the wall, ceiling, wherever. They glow all night."

He's reading the back of the package now. "Create your own galaxy on your bedroom ceiling."

For the first time, Chrissie looks at me, grinning, the black rectangle where his tooth used to be like some soft, daring invitation.

"This is it, you're sure? Where she lives?" I am remembering Ted's pessimistic appraisal about safety in places like this.

"Her dad's place, yeah."

"Would you prefer I wait in the truck?"

"No. C'mon."

Her child's face round and sullen through the screen, Vernice poses with the baby, passive emblem of reproach.

Chrissie, his hair shifting against his naked shoulders, a St. Christopher medal glinting around his neck, addresses her through the screen.

"Hey, babe. Surprise, surprise. *¿Que andan haciendo?* Can we come in?"

Her eyes slew suspiciously to me.

"Oh, she gave me a ride." He hoists the purple bag, bounces it a little. "Got a present for the baby."

She turns her back, walks a few steps. We still see the white block of her blouse through the screen.

Taking this for permission, Chrissie opens the screen door.

Following him in, feeling extraneous, a loose article of sorts, I perch on the couch, an old car seat with chrome armrests, covered with a Mexican blanket. I sit under the balding chin of a mule deer's head, screwed to walnut paneling. Across the room, a morose elk stares beyond me, its muscular, molting neck craned toward the door. Beneath the antlered elk is a TV set. Vernice has been watching soap operas. Now the actors' mouths spring open and closed like fish, their gestures made farcical by silence.

Chrissie's jouncing the baby behind Vernice's hard back.

"Oooh cute, how cute, *mi hija*, my little darling."

The baby, a miniature pink bow Scotch-taped to her fuzzed head, blandly regards her delinquent father.

He acts as though he and Vernice are carrying on a mutually
amiable conversation. He talks, leaves generous blanks for her
to reply. When she doesn't, he keeps going. Vernice holds to
the living-room side of the Formica counter, clutching the
baby like a stuffed animal, her wary eyes on Chrissie.

"So the old man's still parked here . . . how's Flavio doing?
Mind if I look for munchies?" He slings open the refrigerator,
looking at me over its green door ". . . something to drink?
Pepsi, Orange Crush, beer?" He brings out a cheese slice, un-
peels it, stuffs the orange flap in his mouth. "Jail food stinks. I
work in the kitchen, it's disgusting, worse than worst." He
stuffs down three slices in quick succession before coming out
of the kitchen to nuzzle at Vernice.

"Mmm, you feel good, babe" — his hands intimate, cupping her stomach — "gots a love handle, huh." She wears
black spandex shorts. "Mmmm" — he belches — "gots some
baby fat, that's okay, mmm." He keeps it up, kissing her neck,
massaging her belly, his hands seductive.

That does it, the baby fat comment. She answers in Spanish
with a malignant curse. Chrissie backs off, arms flung against
an invisible cross.

"Hey, why are you throwing a drag? I busted out just to see
you, I brought a present for the baby. Here. Next time, if you
want, if that's what it is, I'll bring something for you."

She whacks the small package out of his hand.

"So what, Vernice? What is your fucking problem?"

"You. You're the fucking problem."

I retrieve my Glow-in-the-Dark Stars from the carpet. Vernice is crying now, and I am getting this weird sense, maybe

from the mute soap opera, we're all yoked into some script. I walk to the window and see two men in a dirt field hauling on a mule, on a dead mule. Both men climb onto the hood of a rusted car, drag the mule up onto the rounded hood by its back legs. Laurel and Hardy minus amusement. I look out the window, hearing Vernice's every word, how after every sentence, she sucks in, her breath a tiny, anxious wheeze. I wonder if she has asthma.

The baby looks nonplussed, her eyes limpid, almost blank. My cue nearly missed, I go to Vernice.

"Can I hold her for you?" My arms are outstretched. "What's her name?" Chrissie never said, I wonder if he knew.

"Deliah."

"Okay. Well. Deliah and I will stay in here, watch TV together, while you guys go outside and talk, be by yourselves. Right, baby? Deliah and I'll watch TV."

Out the trailer's south window we watch the two men in loose overalls set fire to the mule on top of the car. We watch the mule burn, the car burn. Out the north window, we see Vernice, stomping up and down the potholed driveway, yelling and crying. I flip Deliah the opposite direction, toward the TV. Vernice is yelling "fuck" every third or fourth word. I don't hear anything from Chrissie, as if the earlier situation, in the trailer, has reversed. We check on our burning mule, and when we get back, I watch Vernice smacking Chrissie, who doesn't defend himself. I don't know why, but I remember Ted's keys in the ignition, and with Deliah jouncing on my shoulder, I run. Chrissie's already in the truck, revving the new engine, spinning the new tires, spewing out mud shrapnel, roaring onto the thin dirt road, a damned idiot in Ted's truck.

One hand clamped to Deliah's bottom, the other steadying her neck, I run down the road, see Chrissie screech the truck around, gun it warlike toward Vernice, who walks squarely the other way, her white, reproachful back a target. He aims the truck like a hunk of artillery, flying straight toward her.

On pure theatric instinct, I step with the baby into the center of the road, replacing one target for another. After he swerves, I walk up to the stalled, skidded truck.

"Hey, light-foot. Get down and hold your baby girl. You haven't even held her yet."

It takes a while but he gets down from Ted's truck, lifts his daughter from me, carries her to the trailer steps. I back the truck into the yard.

We sit on the steps, defeated, until I, having read a great many books with printed instructions on crisis, start thinking like a therapist.

"Chrissie. What is it you want?"

He doesn't answer.

"Chrissie. Can you tell me? What is it you want?"

"To be left alone."

"Isn't there anyone you care about?"

"My daughter."

"What about Vernice?"

No answer.

"Would it help if you saw a counselor?"

He shrugs. "Last time I got busted, we saw one."

"How was that?"

"She blamed everything on me."

"What about Vernice's dad?"

"We used to hunt together." Chrissie is on his feet so fast, I think he's forgotten Deliah so I lift her from him. He looks completely dangerous.

"Bullshit. Who needs this fucking bullshit, man."

"What about Vernice?"

"Fuck her. Hey, drive me to the warehouse. I need to get my stuff."

"Where are you going?"

"Salt Lake. Denver. Disneyland. Back to jail, that's where."

He ignores whatever I lamely say, pulls himself into the truck and sits waiting on the passenger side.

Vernice reappears in the driveway, in her father's territory.

"She's beautiful," I say, handing Deliah back and giving Vernice twenty dollars. "From Chrissie, for diapers."

She pockets my money, desperate to think so, and stares at Chrissie, viciously focused on nothing.

"God, Vernice. That mule smells terrible."

She holds her baby, circling her hand on the little quiet back, stolid like hers.

"Yeah, well my dad and his friend are kind of crazy. They do stuff like that sometimes."

When we get back to the warehouse, it's dark though still hot, still windy. I unlock the office, and there is a half-wistful phone message from Ted . . . was I surprised to get the roses, he hoped I'd had a good day, a safe day, he loved and adored me, he'd be home before noon, where was I.

I walk outside, back to the crate, willing to drive Chrissie wherever he wants, Los Angeles, Salt Lake, back to Chacón and Vernice or back to Springer. There's no answer, so I push in, burrowing my flashlight in one corner, where it makes a manger light. On the sleeping bag, Chrissie is combing his hair with Vernice's blue-handled comb.

"Can I sit with you?"

No answer.

On an impulse I won't call honorable or good, I take from my back pocket the joke for Ted, the gift for Deliah. I stick a star in the center of my forehead. Pry up another and use my thumb to stick it on Chrissie's forehead. I am a sower of celestial grain, comets, moons and half-moons lighting our shadowed faces. Chrissie switches off the flashlight, while I plant a luminous galaxy on his smooth, warm chest. He lifts off my T-shirt and with careful fingers seeds a realm of sallow stars over my breasts.

The heavens are used up. We crouch in the black, airless crate, jewels and miracles, our faces glittering like Eulogia's palms, gloried like Holman's Jesus. And when my nature, which distrusts joy, makes its pathetic move to ruin us, when I try awfully hard to make him touch me, Chrissie, out of integrity, or indifference or some measure in between I'll never know, won't do it, won't touch me in ways that would start off one thing and destroy everything else.

I drive him more than halfway to Springer. But first, on our way out of town, I point to the dead Indian. He laughs, saying he'd fooled Ted that way once, had Ted believing a rotten, rolled-up blanket was a dead Indian. I see Chrissie for what will be the last time, reaching back into the truck to grab his stuff, and thanking me, a viridescent tail of comet igniting his beautiful mouth, his broken teeth.

Some months after our wedding, I am, of all this world's homely activities, mixing meat loaf, my hands sticky, glued in meat and eggs, when Ted calls. I listen to the machine, my wrists chapped and flecked with meat, wincing at another of my husband's awful jokes, before I understand it isn't.

Chrissie's motorcycle had slid into a wet mountain curve, struck a phone pole, his head had come apart from his body, sailing over a fence into a field of alfalfa. He'd been grading roads for the Forest Service, living with Vernice and the baby, working hard. There was a rosary at seven. We should go. Where was I . . .

Somewhere far from a devoted husband's faith in me.

My cold fingers, speckled red with grains of meat, remember here and here and here, stiffly touch the hundred places where small, store-bought stars brightened the dark crate we played in, loosened its makeshift coffin, slowed to nothing our hopeful, half-broken, unsimple hearts.

The Good and Faithful Widow

We pick here because death is life's ornament, because the place is masculine without the compromising presence of a male. It is a fortress, really, and in it we play as children, infected, set subtly adrift in our Father's body.

We are a fortress vacant of femininity, apart from Lita's wavering beauty, the arcane threshold beauty of a fourteen-year-old girl.

More to the point, to give you comforting reference, we live in a historically valuable, nineteenth-century adobe compound, walled in, the vast courtyard at its center marred by skeletal tumbleweed and a crumbling Moorish fountain. The previous owner, a homosexual architect of conflicting reputation, gutted the lightless, mudded interior; it is now pristine and meticulous as a yacht, empty of female resonance down to the dominant alabaster urinals in the skylit bathrooms, and the kitchen sink, aluminum and deep enough to pose in. The realtor, a militant grandmother in dour olive, informed us our guest apartment had been a Spanish *morada,* meeting place of the Penitente brotherhood — thus the oppressive distillate of male spirits I felt there, the monastic hive's dark hum.

Lita and I have been here awhile, content I think. We know no one but each other and our life is sweetly routine. Lita rides to school on her bicycle each morning, I walk to the town library, where I volunteer. Most afternoons, we swim at the indoor community pool, which is very nearly always empty.

My child's beauty is mainly incorrupt because she has not yet acknowledged or learned to use it; when she swims alongside me in her watery corridor, like some blurred, pale iris dragged by spring currents, I would nearly compare her to the myriad angels I collect. Yet angels are ungendered, and Lita belongs to that most fertile, least accessible territory of goddesses, Innocence.

My collection, displayed, of angels suggests an ambition to ungender myself. To martyr my genitals. At a certain point in one's life, I believe the sacrifice is welcomed and therefore no sacrifice. I wish to be neutered and ambitious beyond my own residual charms. I am done, I tell Lita, if not in a chant, certainly with monotonous repetition, I am finished with husbands, lovers, fathers, brothers. At times, self-pity creeps in, meaning I am not done at all, only lonely.

Lita tests me. (I have always encouraged her to do so.)

— Then why are you Catholic, why worship a masculine trinity?

— *Because death is life's ornament, and I regret your father's death by this decade's peculiar sexual plague, a plague having everything to do with the discreet and desperate sale of this house. Because my duty is to keep you safe in the cradle of naïveté until I say so, until I say so, until I say it is safe to cross the street without my hand, to swim unguarded in waters above your precious head.*

— Because in ways I am responsible.

*

Lita and I, who discuss everything as equals, agree to hire someone to live in the morada apartment, to maintain our things for us, help us with our everyday lives. A housekeeper. I unbolt the courtyard gates. A primitive figure swathed in gray fleece mimics the snow, somber and marbled with mud, heaped to either side of her. She wears a hairy white cap with a flagrant pom-pom, her own hair, I surmise, plastered beneath the cap, its white rim an Italianate halo or whipping of tired flagella about her mottled face. A thin, desultory snow flecks the space between us, causing me to imagine we are two odd figures trapped inside a domed, water-filled children's toy, most often a holiday scene.

I invite her into the main house, resolved to inspect character, question work habits, audition her for this ill-defined part of Housekeeper.

I am often pleasurably hypnotized by another's vulgarity. This was certainly true in the case of my husband. As this silver, porpoise-shaped creature squats in my aggressive white kitchen, in my bold, linearly efficient kitchen, squatting like a tin lump, I devolve into a sort of happy paralysis.

— Ask me my real name, she repeats.

— Irene, isn't that correct, that's what I was told at the library . . .

— Arthur Vargas, she yelps, hoisting her sweatshirt under her chin, holding it there, her cloddish face boastful. Two speckled, cigarish breasts flop, nearly touching her girdled pear of a stomach. Oh. These are comically exaggerated, burlesque breasts, horrifyingly incorrect beside the thick wrists netted with dense, messy black hairs.

— Starting when I was ten, I wanted to be a girl. I let my hair grow long. I've had five different operations in Colorado. They kept operating until I ran out of money. I'm only half-done, half-finished.

(How evident: the granite stubble, its clipped dark turf thicketing up from under the orange pancake makeup.)

When she asks, I indicate the small bathroom nearby. Irene keeps up talking, the door flung wide as she makes her noises, urgent and unperturbed as a cow or horse. In the month Irene/Arthur was with us, I never knew her to be anything but incomprehensibly cheerful and openhanded as wealthy people are assumed to be but seldom are. In an ironic, retrospective sense, Irene approached my ideal, childlike, joyfully neutered (in her case one set of genitals quite literally knocking the other one out).

My child, home from school, stands in the doorway, a gold and ivoried marzipan, a confectionery swan.

— Oh Lita, this person is androgynous. Biologically liberated. Imagine.

— Ish, Mother, Lita sighs, cracking open the restaurant-size refrigerator door, hunting around for one of her interminable vanilla yogurts; you are bored, aren't you?

I took on Irene with perverse fascination and fraudulent motive, and if it is simpleminded, too easy a target, I still insist Lita's change for the worse began soon after. People are celestial chemistries, after all, and Irene's tainted elements provoked my daughter into exhibiting symptoms. When she was three, Lita came down with chicken pox, one peppermint speck at a time, one, then dozens, candied her white skin, until the whole feverish body was blotched and unseemly, suffering. Since Irene has begun keeping house for us, Lita's symptoms are exactly similar, faint, singular, then cumulative and finally disastrous. Between us, silences now thump out like measured bolts of stiff yardage, conversation fails, stifled by resentment, rebellion, who knows what.

My darling. Newly, irrationally conscious of three young men in chairs beside the pool, lifeguards, Lita swaddles herself in a baby blue towel, minces in hobbled steps to the pool's edge, deftly slips out, like some delicacy from a wrapper, into the pool. Worse, she now refuses to change into her suit or come out of the dressing rooms, staying in that dank, greenish place, playing solitaire, wearing baggy, shapeless clothes until I return from my swim, resolutely cheerful. Here I am, released by my body's imperfections, so legion as to force me into indifference over anybody's opinion of it . . . my physical deterioration yielding the unexpected virtue of freedom from caring what three young men by a pool might think, just as my physically splendid daughter skulks, fully clothed, in a mildewed shower stall, snapping down card after card in a compulsive, ordained pattern.

I am a weak person. My nature submits to any personality perverse and dominant enough. This was certainly true in the case of my husband. And though I am working on this weakness in myself, still, I welcome Irene at my front door each day, knowing I will listen helplessly to her prurient exploits, hang on like someone ravenous . . . until she concludes her work by heating up a can of alphabet soup, that peculiar sweaty stink of tinned soup as provocative as any romantic atmosphere.

I never ask Irene what she does in her free hours. They are hers. My pity breeds an insidious, false sense of superiority though it is a relief to pity someone besides myself, slighted by a child for whom solitude and privacy have become luxurious and coveted concepts; while for me, they are incarcerations.

I step up my activities in the San Francisco De Asis parish by volunteering for jail ministry. On Thursday evenings, I drive to the town jail to assist with mass, while Lita stays home to answer an increasing number of personal telephone calls, taken in sullen monotones.

How justifiably morose and vain are the young!

Our routine is damaged. I trail Irene about, helping her move rugs, pieces of furniture, lending her extra money, asking advice about Lita, over whom I have become like some spurned, mopish suitor; as her popularity with persons named Robin, Aki, Phoenix and August increases (all curiously asexual names), her communication with me inversely dwindles to curbed, reluctant responses.

And this idea of baggy, misshapen clothes! I'll see Lita off for school in one of the expensive outfits I'd helped her choose before we moved here, and she'll bike home in something bizarre, a huge, faded college shirt, torn leggings . . . some squalid orphan getup from Dickens.

I snuck into her room one night, to lift up the white eyelet comforter and pinch her leg, to test how bony, how possibly anorexic . . . but her flesh was rounded, rosy, edible, and instead of holding the lantern over the beast I beheld forbidden, perfect beauty.

One afternoon when the library was closed for Presidents'
Day, I searched through Lita's room . . . like an ardent detec-
tive . . . discovering notes, dozens of notes creased into elegant
origami birds, clever flowers. Unfolding each one, I read ob-
scene, sluttish trash . . . girls confiding in Lita, appealing as if
she were an oracle in these matters, such an appalling, whorish
rush of heat, actual or conjured, I couldn't tell.

I devoted myself. I cooked Lita's childhood favorites, which
she disdained though prettily, so as not to offend me. Giving
Irene money to fix her station wagon, writing to her mother in
Albuquerque (Irene neither reads nor writes). The solicitous
servant whose misery is undetected, pathological.

While Irene/Arthur Vargas, ever flagrant in her happy stories of having been a madam in a small-town brothel, for all
her shameless concupiscence and gluttonous triumph at having contorted her body into a double-genitaled freak of nature, was as closed to me as Lita. As if they were in some collu-
sion or conspiracy not so much against me as necessarily
excluding me. Exclusion, a terrifying word.

My respite is in the library, among perished authors, their
spirits tamped in homely black ciphers upon the page, and
still-living authors, shut willingly up in blocks, in cool, regi-
mented neighborhoods.

The church, San Francisco De Asis my second refuge. The
robed, compassionate priest, the monogamous servers of the
host (its ivoried planet upon my tongue!), the stealthy celibate
children, my sexless angels.

In jail, where mass is celebrated on the free side of the bars,
I wring compassion from myself like a sponge, trying to scrub

down the cell with it. This jail resembles a Fisher-Price toy, like the ones Lita's father used to buy her, barns and schools and airports bought out of guilt and remorse, motives a child can't see for their ruinous subtlety.

The communal cell is windowless cinder block, painted white, the first time white impressed me as an evil color.

Standing close beside the priest, I read aloud from the missalette, "Cursed is the man who trusts in human beings, who seeks his strength in flesh, whose heart turns away from the Lord. He is like a barren bush in the desert that enjoys no change of season, but stands in a lava waste, a salt and empty earth . . ." I read aloud to the white cement walls, the white bars with the scarlet lock, read to the white floors with fat scarlet lines and fat arrows going this way and that like a child's game board, read to the brown plaid couch, the plywood bookshelf with Reader's Digest Condensed Books and stale magazines, read aloud to the sludge-colored TV and to six prisoners in construction-paper orange suits, chunky Fisher-Price figures, their feet in Oriental, black rubber thongs.

The priest is a young man, newly ordained and a flashy dresser. Under the apple green brocade surplice, his suede cowboy boots stick out. His earnest face sweats. In costly western wear, he preaches to the prisoners, all of whom are Hispanic like himself, on the worthiness of poverty, the blessings of insult, the woe to come to the rich and the replete, who will scatter like chaff into nothingness.

A fine fish to fry! Irene has been arrested for selling beer and wine out of her newly repaired station wagon on Sunday, yesterday. She has asked to see me.

We find the second key, Lita and I, and like guilty snoops, unlock the small morada door. First impression, the place is suspiciously neat. We look but find no wine bottles, no beer cans, nothing. Maybe the police confiscated everything, Lita suggests breathlessly. Neither of us has ever had anything like this happen to us.

In the bathroom, we stand before various tubes and bags, strange apparatus hanging from the shower rod, so resonant with sexual disturbance we do not know what to say. On a dressing table near the bed, we look, as if upon curious speci-mens, at depilatory devices and creams, a theatrical mirror with bare pink bulbs stuck around it, raw heaps of makeup, base, powder, lipsticks, rouges, eyeshadows . . . On the bed, a kimono like a crushed, red insect. On the windowsill, perfume bottles hold light like paste jewels. The erotic clumsily com-bats a subversive odor of male. The place is haunted, we both feel it.

Lita slips her narrow feet into a pair of red silk embroidered slippers, roomy and daddy-size on her delicate feet. Humon-gous, she whispers, rising on her toes.

I leave her memorizing Shakespeare at the cold white kitchen table, waiting for someone named Robin to come over and help her. I think I smell wine on Lita's breath, but decide I am wrong.

On the free side of the communal cell where we say mass, the room is empty except for a heavyset man, his orange back to me, sitting on the plaid couch, watching TV. I lean against the washing machine to wait. After a while, I walk through the booking room and into the small, fluorescent-lit, windowless office, hardly different from the cell, where two policemen sit at gray desks.

— Where is Irene Vargas? May I see her?

The thinner policeman laughs. Arthur? He's been in there since dinner, waiting for you. I went through grade school with Vargas, poor messed-up dude's always had this thing for thinking he's a girl.

I notice a *Penthouse* magazine on the other policeman's desk.

I go back, stand beside the white bars. Irene.

The man watching TV turns.

Inches apart, we stare at one another. She is a mountain of humiliation. They have shaved her hair to match the stubble on her bare face.

— Could you bring my makeup, my stuff. I'm losing it in here.

Except for the grainy crescent of beard above the genderless orange, Irene's moony face is a communion host, secret, opaque, monstrous.

I talk to the thinner policeman about going home to get some things for my housekeeper. I ask how much money to release her on bail.

As I am leaving, putting on my coat, he says, "No razors."

— What?

— You can't give Arthur razors. He'll kill himself.

— He's been here before?

— Arthur Vargas? I've lost count. Like I tell you, he's a piece of work. Leonard here, he's always kind of had a crush on him, right, Leonard?

*

When I get home, vain, pinkish light comes from the morada, from Irene/Arthur's apartment, while across the courtyard, the kitchen lights are on but I don't see Lita. Leaving the wooden gates unbolted, I move stealthily into a thick clump of bladed iris beneath one of the windows, ornate ironwork across its glass, the effect like spying through a black veil . . .

My eyes water, my feet are numb in the raw, tarry mud, the courtyard is a ghostly square, shabby with weeds and stubborn islands of grim snow, the deteriorated fountain rising repellent in its center.

Someone blocks my vision, stands directly in front of me, then moves farther into the room as if receding. From the back, this person of indeterminate sex has a long, brown ponytail, is tall and egret-slender in the red kimono.

Lita is sitting cross-legged on the bed, very close to me. The figure in the kimono turns, arms flung, red sleeves winglike, the face ethereal, amoral. He smiles directly at me, that is impossible, he must be smiling at my daughter. This boy begins to gesture melodramatically, an arm flung this way, then that, the head tilting limply, the face malleable, at once compelling and utterly foolish. I cannot bear him.

My mother steps briskly out of me and goes to the door, knocks hard.

— I've come to get Irene's things, good heavens, what are you two doing? What game is this? Out, at once!

But I am rooted to the barred window, an ugly plant thrusting unseasonably from the dormant iris. From my post of concealed privilege, I persist in watching, find solace, watching.

When the door abruptly opens, I crouch down, unseen.

They walk toward the house, playfully reciting lines, Hamlet, Ophelia, Hamlet, Ophelia. Children. Still so.

In mud-drowned shoes, I enter, kneel in the dark apartment to the broken body of Irene/Arthur, kneel to my child's innocence, my daughter's innocence, kneel for myself, gone into spiritual pride and a profound, corrupting loneliness.

After Lita and I were again by ourselves, without a house-keeper, we went to the pool. Lita kept to the dressing room while I swam, diligent, compulsive, the nearest form of happiness for me, when Lita unexpectedly walked out, unflinching as a goddess, setting her bare feet resolutely then diving, her splendid form hung in light, before vanishing beneath water smelling unnaturally of clay.

If Schopenhauer were alive, I, the good and faithful widow, would blindfold and spin him three times, unmask him and say, "Okay about your patterns, your ideas of fate and fixed patterns in a life, what about this then, what about this, how about this?"

Revelations of Child Love
for the Soul of Dame Mi Mah

IN SIXTEEN SHEWINGS

BY BODILY SIGHT

BY WORD SIGHT

BY GHOSTLY SIGHT

REVELATION THE FIRST: Untenured professor, damp-winged peripheral, I bring Dame Mi Mah to the university, where she has difficulty getting on and off the tram, falls in the library, and I am shocked by her decline. I hold office hours, two of them, in my anchorite's hoosegow, a negative enclosure, the voice from its walls: no visitors for me.

Mi Mah wanders off to shop, in scarlet boy-shorts, rump a flat little red play block, shoulders hunched under an expensive blouse as if to say she requires more than the gold breastplate which is her jewelry and defense. I will say this. Dame Mi Mah, though served unjustly, moves sturdily and well, stumps with politic vigor through the indifferent terrain of Old.

REVELATION THE SECOND: A common butterfly scooped from the pool this morning, drowned on blue netting until I peeled up its silken flanges, black with yellow barring, its antennae, bulbed at the tips like a bobby pin, set it flickering, repentant, on an overturned brick by the clothesline. I had retrieved life. It mattered a great deal. This occurred to me as, through the dirty glass of the sliding door, I saw Dame Mi Mah, in her saffron kimono, flecking about the cool, sparse enclosure of my rented house, what I call the Sanitorium.

REVELATION THE THIRD, IN WHICH THE PREVIOUS MATTER IS RESTATED: After her fall in the library, among books of criticism, I find Mi Mah dropped on a stone bench, wholesome youth brawling past, hale collegiates with polished limbs, vibrant voices, infallible strides. She bends, blots with Kleenex a string of blood from the cut on her shin, loathing her old, see-through skin, dryly mapped as wings. I nearly say, hold steady, you are become the Invisible Woman, but give her, rather, directions to town, two blocks left, one right, you can do it, yes, stand watchful as the blood-bright shorts, the turtle-hunch, the hair a thready halo, wander off, dearest Mi Mah, riffling through her purse, patting pockets, adjusting this, that, so busy, absorbed in her busyness, plucking at the solitary self, the irreparable instrument. What will she buy?

REVELATION THE FOURTH: Although it is October in Arizona, and the pool is icy as a mountain lake, Mi Mah steps forth, (the dog prancing behind her on two ruffed circus legs), in her black suit, nosegays of purple violets strewn across it, three flounces around the seat, a girly swimtog. Tugging on a white rubber cap, Mi Mah determinedly plunks in. Showing off, I plunge ambitiously back and forth, scarcely breathing; and after her obsessive chatter of health and exercise, she must do what she does, which is to get in and plug away on her back, arms wheeling, head slightly lifted, a plucky marshmallow. The dog, yipping convulsively at pool's edge, snaps at her white head as it goes by, dropping his blue rubber newspaper, *The Daily Growl,* into the pool as she shoves by again. The dog adores Mi Mah, who complains the next day, her arm aches from hurtling *The Daily Growl* around the overgrown yard.

REVELATION FIFTH: A Sears dryer? she offers. Oh no, I demur, a new sofa would be best. There's a clothesline in Arizona, all anyone needs, a white line to stiffen and bake the clothes, hang the sheets and towels, all caulked with Sonoran light. In the furniture store, we whisper, as if in a museum or perhaps a mortuary, in any case, the lighting is ominously dull, there are no signs of life in the vacant living rooms, family rooms, bedrooms, the silent dozens of rooms. Mi Mah hustles through the subdued labyrinth, while I, slowed to torpor by such a dollhouse maze, lag. I finally spy the little figure, the beloved red block and white hunch, flitting spectrally through a colonial cherry-wood bedroom.

Mi Mah, I wail, frightened at having lost her in this mock catacomb.

A SIXTH REVELATION, WHEREIN DAME MI MAH AN-SWERS BY WAY OF SPONTANEOUS EULOGY: Q: What would you miss if he were gone? (Can't say dead, Mi Mah has aversions to both word and subject, eliminating much fine literature and serious film.)

He's a great cuddler, I'll say that for Jack. When we golf on Tuesdays and Thursdays, he says, Show 'em, Tiger, just when I swing. He's a tease, calls me Butterball or Slim, and in bed, says my nose drills a cold hole in his back. He's never beat me or abused me in any way. Your father's a generous man.

SEVENTH REVELATION, WHEREIN A REMINISCENCE OCCURS IN YET ANOTHER DIM-LIT PLACE, A RESTAURANT WITH A WESTERN THEME WHERE WE ORDER IDENTICALLY PINKENED CLUMPS OF BEEF: I've told you, my childhood, Pete's sake. Dull as a dream. Johnny Bauer, first kiss. Paul Faldesack (the name!), first boyfriend, Margaret Fitzgerald married him, poor doof. Hayrides in winter, hot chocolate. Mother loved throwing parties, used to go all out. Our Lady of Angels Elementary, then Mercy High. Cortez, same street we lived on when you were little. Imagine. What did I think about becoming? A nurse. Always used to say I was going to visit my daddy in Davenport. No one knew what it meant, but I'd pack my cardboard suitcase and wait in a homemade gauze tent under our big willow. Hours of waiting.

She had more shoes than anything, your grandmother. Loved to garden, she stuck this big snowball bush by the back door, you had to fight past it to get outside. With her arthritis, she finally couldn't wear all those fancy shoes. Your Great Gramma McGuire fixed me coffee with milk, took me to see Mrs. Wiggs of the Cabbage Patch. Grampa slapped on the lilac vegetal aftershave, puffed big, rum-soaked cigars on the back porch. Aunt Mabel? Oh, his sister, never cared much about her. Somebody claimed we came down from Wild Bill Hickok, don't know who. Write everything down for you?

Hell's bells. I've told you all this time and again. Special? No, I never was special to anyone.

REVELATION EIGHT, THE NARRATOR'S HASTY CON-FESSION: Hypochondria — glorious affliction! This week I have cancer. Three types. Breast, cervix, ovary. My sexual symptoms are evident. The last doctor I saw, a Doctor Ting, jaundiced, lean as a greyhound, I told this Doctor Ting, as he fiddled with a light inside me, the body is a fooler, isn't it, all symmetry on the outside, the inside a mess of planets and angles and shiftings, chaotic textures and jarring colors. Mister Rogers, the children's television friend, sings, something like this — "Boys are fancy on the outside, girls are fancy on the inside." What can he mean? Are we misled by the seemliness of our outsides into expecting an equivalent symmetry in the universe, and why are we never permitted a peek at our interiors? (This calls to mind the Museum of Science and Industry in Chicago, where I once saw, in a little-used hallway, slices of humans, one man, one woman, both identified, both black, you could tell by the outer rind, sliced like a roll of lunch meat or those tree circles, entombed in plastic, presumably so visitors could glimpse someone else's interior if not their own. These disks of human flesh were intricate, astonishing, faded stepping-stones.)

Hypochondria works like this: Should you allay suspicion over one ailment, you can swiftly substitute another, for the body brilliant is host to infinite petty breakdown. The headache of high blood pressure translates into the rash of syphilis, the back pain of the kidney becomes the nether pain of obstructed colon, and so on. I devour medical texts in libraries, in bookstores, the stack beneath my bed is memorized; nights pass busily for the hypochondriac, which is perhaps the point. What I am not permitted to see is what is most real.

NINTH REVELATION: True. This is true. Mother keeps a Baggie of Fig Newtons in her makeup kit. One a day does it, she giggles. She has given me a small, greasy bottle of Aura-Glow, from the Edgar Cayce Foundation. Yesterday I found her spraddled on the bed, legs akimbo, rubbing her stomach in slow circles. What are you doing, I asked. She looked so composed, ritualistic. Following directions from a magazine article. Circling reduces abdominal fat. Mother jogs, bicycles, has practiced yoga, swims, walks. She can wolf down four pieces of cake at one sitting. She is not consistent, which saddens me.

TENTH REVELATION, IN WHICH NOISE SHE MAKES LEADS TO SMALL CONCLUSIONS: The first thing I experience when she arrives is SOUND. Flinging wide all the windows, chattering incessantly then slip slap slip slap down the hallways into every room like cannon, artillery, short bursts of rubber thongs. I am afraid to look at them the whole time she is here, their hard rubber birdshot noise frightens me.

REVELATION ELEVEN, COMPARISON OF MODESTIES: The astonishing new thing about Mi Mah is her savage immodesty. The first morning, I locate her in a crotch-high T-shirt in the backyard, hosing, for some reason, the sidewalk rather than watering the roses or the orange trees, tipped way over so her purple Jockey shorts show. Next she hangs out clothes on the perfect white line, saying lookee, I have the same bra, hoisting the T-shirt so I can view the identical bra, lookee upon seventy-four-year-old nakedness. This glare of original flesh I was expelled from half a century ago stuns me. My body's consistently tricked me, I've learned to conceal its accumulation of scars, cysts, veins, wens, hairs, enshroud myself in prudish lengths of obscuring materials, while she jaunts naked, she would say, as a jaybird, a partially clothed jaybird, around my damask green, citrus-smelling yard.

(I know a gentleman who must clip his mother-in-law's toenails Sunday evenings, a disciple at her yellow clay feet. I know a woman who cannot leave her mother past three days; her eyelashes grow into her eyes, and only this woman can trim the old mother's lashes properly.)

I am terrified of Dame Mi Mah's body, cavorting and bony, its macabre vigor, all the girth at the center, a pesky increase she variously slaps at, circles ritually, or sweets-feeds with all manner of candies, cakes, jellies, fig cookies.

REVELATION TWELVE: A MIGHTY DESIRE TO RECEIVE THREE THOUGHT-WOUNDS: The body as negative corral or crypt, the body as theologic hospital, the body as pot or womb, sloshing up all manner of stew, spontaneous corruptions, purifications.

REVELATION THIRTEEN: WOUNDS RECEIVED BY WAY OF MEMORY IN A MATTER OF HOURS: I collapse, exhausted, on the new sofa. I am probably ill, certainly I am ill. Mi Mah is in the kitchen, noisy, half or more naked. Pots slam, cabinets open and water runs in short vehement bursts.

When I waken, the room is dark. Rich light comes from the kitchen, the rich familiar smell of her cooking, of the foods she has always cooked in the familiar ways she has always cooked them. For the sweetest minute, dear as blood, I am little, full of faith, little and cared for, nourished by a new mother working her family's tender acre to yield, over time, its fated portion of bliss and the rest.

During my last wedding, she yakked like a parrot in the most sacred parts, she poked me in the eye while making the sign' of the cross. At the reception, she refused to dance, ate piece after piece of almond wedding cake, looking absent-minded yet stuffed with foreboding.

This morning I slugged her, slugged her in the arm, to stop her from jabbing everybody, an irritating habit she has always had. There, I said, does that feel like fun? I couldn't look at Mi Mah's face, it would have been awful to see what I had done, smacking her that way.

FOURTEENTH REVELATION: THE MOTHER TONGUE:

Flapdoodle
Holy catastrophe
Bibble di bobble di boop
Yee gawds
Scat before I knock you six ways to Sunday (to the dog)
Whoopdidoo
Pete's sake
Hell's bells
Cripes

Holy Toledo
Oh spit!

FIFTEENTH REVELATION, THE FOURTH WOUND MADE MANIFEST: There are cysts in the ovary that attain great size, grapefruits, cantaloupes, larger melons, nature's blunderings toward a child. When delivered surgically into glare, they show themselves possessed of teeth, hair, bone, bits of ear. I feel, under my bloated abdomen, there exists one of these melons with teeth and hair, its eye turned inward and grieving.

A SIXTEENTH REVELATION, WHERE MINOR CATAS-TROPHE DISTRACTS FROM THAT MOST HOLY TRIAL FOR WHICH WE CAN NEVER BE TOO PREPARED: On the morning she is to leave, Mother and I take ourselves around the block, exercising ourselves and the dog, who carries his green leash in his mouth, trotting himself absurdly. Forgetting my glasses, I am blind to everything but the single, pampas grass plume smoking up from what looks to be the roof of my rented house. Good god, the house is on fire, I shout to Mi Mah, stumbling toward it and hearing her behind me, I didn't leave anything on, I didn't leave anything on. Several boys idle on the sidewalk, gawking. Boys, what's burning? One turns with no emotion, a car. Yes, he's right. A Volkswagen bus, the same blue color as my house, is oddly in flames in front of my driveway. Mother and I are frightened to walk around it to get into the house. What if it explodes? We are very excited, standing like children in the street as the fire engine arrives, Mi Mah dressed for her plane trip in what she calls her Mother Superior suit, dark navy, tailored and severe . . . (more and more her clothes resemble costumes to which she affixes names — Nurse Nancy, Mother Superior, etc., all part of her history in some way). The final image I have, she stands in the broad driveway, one wrist oddly flapped as if to mimic a homosexual stereotype, and chattering in a feverish, high-pitched voice to the firemen, none of whom is listening, busy, of course, with their fire. I call to her. Mother Superior! Mommy! Who are you talking to? No one's listening.

Before leaving the airport, I will purchase a plastic egg planted with cactus seeds, a transparent pencil loaded with desert pebbles, and a glassy tequila lollipop with a real tequila worm embedded in it, trinkets I would have trumpeted for and wept to have as a child and never received. But before any of that, I will stand nose to nose with Mi Mah's bright rudder of a face, watch it transfigure with adoration for her old child, so wildly and so devotedly trying to hold fast the gate against wolves, who are, after all, part of the plan, mostly natural and divine agents of conversion.

Still. Under my bed. Where truth lies. A text memorized:

At the bird market. What power, what determination in these tiny frantic bodies! Life resides in this bit of nothing which animates a tuft of matter, and which nonetheless emerges from matter itself and perishes with it. But the perplexity remains: impossible to explain this fever this per-

petual dance, this representation, this spectacle which life
affords itself. What a theater, breath!

— E. M. CIORAN

You first, Old Mommy.
Wear whatever you like.
Red shorts for courage?
Age before beauty?
Death before dishonor?
So they say.

Hallie

Filthy white Impala, stinking of sweet gardenia like a prom. Flopped on the vinyl front seat, Hallie feels light like murder on the heel of her face, pushes up to look in back. One rear window is cranked, she can see Bluebird, cross-legged on the rim of the gorge, a tiny monk, preternaturally contained for a child of five. Her entire nervous system clunks, oh but she refuses alarm, refuses any negative thing. Nothing to acknowledge but fabricated calm. Dumping her past, wind bailing it out the car windows, trashing roadsides from Cheyenne to here, nothing acknowledged but uncolored calm. Sometimes, doing one thing dangerous, sublimely out of character, the body steps in with a massive, hormonal calm.

Bluebird rubs a blue-black rabbit skin up/down up/down one chafed knee.

> I could fly if I wanted.
> How about a drive?
> I hate the car.

Hallie flicks stones down the purplish cleft canyon, into gunky, taupe water flashing dully below, thinks about how much speed a thing gathers, falling.

Well. How about *you* drive?

Me?

Yeah. On my lap. We'll steer together.

The bridge is easy, the big, wingy car moseying. It is the other side, the land on the other side, that is hexed. The Impala starts horse-rodeo stuff, heaving, bucking, Hallie and Bluebird both bashing away at the steering wheel, stop it stop it stop it, get us to town then quit. The car waits for the south end of town before shimmying dead in the road. Three Hispanic men in a green pickup push it into the Pinch Penny Wash O Mat parking lot, where it sits, a downed, chrome-tipped gull.

Must be time to do our laundry.

Hallie navigates with the passive oar of fate, believes there are few accidents. Synchronicity triumphs. Since leaving Cheyenne, they have been living out of the Impala; it is thoroughly trashed with Bluebird's Happy Meal boxes, Hallie's coffee cups and salad trays, a touring garbage heap. Right now, Hallie is pulling what dirty clothes she can find off the floor, out of the cracks of the backseat, yanking clothes like weeds, stuffing them in Bluebird's arms until her skinny chin rests on top like a stopper, a cork.

Okay, heave ho.

Hallie likes the theory laundromat owners are ectoplasmic. You sense their gray, elusive, irritable presence from handwritten signs taped to broken dryers and washers, in runny washroom signs over toilets, no napkins, tampons, etc. She and Bluebird are the only ones in the Pinch Penny except a homely, wide dog, its freckled teats trawling the linoleum. Bluebird had to leave Pickles, her terrier; Hallie promising Rick could ship the dog after they were settled, but how can that happen if they're running away and he isn't supposed to find them? He isn't even Bluebird's father, but a mechanic, a coke head and a dirty drain on her money. The sex had been fantastic, initially cosmic, then a dirtier, faster drain on her heart, so bad she came to understand their relationship probably fell under the term *abuse* though he'd mostly not struck her, only yelled, lied and had other girlfriends, wasn't that enough? She was afraid of him. Someday she'd figure out how she could let herself have great sex with such a lousy individual. Plus she'd keep an eye out for a dog similar to Pickles.

Hallie talks briefly into the pay phone, hangs up, stares intently into the floor, into bones most likely of Indians buried under the foundation of the Laundromat, her hand on the receiver.

Shoot.

What, Moomers?

Damn. Darn.

Hallie runs the list through her head. Things seem past guidance, getting discouraging. Her insides feel like falling cake. Dead car, sixty-five dollars, the one personal friend she had counted on suddenly off to Nicaragua, part of a women's peace brigade. The linkage of events that was supposed to slide her out from under him had snapped. No job, no friend, crapped car. For a weak half-second, she considers going back.

It's okay, Moomers. Can we eat at Lota Burger? I see one right over there.

Nope, nope, final nope. No more junk-food troughs. You

are going to eat a normal ham-and-egg breakfast, bacon and toast, juice and pancakes, whatever.

Then Hallie spots the mechanic's garage across the street, and within minutes, a guy named Roy (from the red, birthday cake script on his shirt pocket) has the Impala's hood up, fiddling in its sullen guts. Hallie has always experienced regrettable, extraordinary lust at the sight of men bending over opened hoods of cars. Regrettable because that's how she'd got into such shit with Rick, the way he'd looked, fixing her car. Thank god this Roy person has no charm, no appeal whatsoever. Doesn't see her or Bluebird as much but objects to benefit him personally, chiefly financial.

Transmission's shot to hell.

So —

Three fifty to get it going or fifty dollars for parts. These 'fifty-nines aren't worth diddly-squat except parts.

Oh.

Foul news. Not true. Rick prized this car. To cover her ignorance, Hallie turns prim.

I'll consider it. Thank you.

You decide. Let me know. Slams the hood and walks back across the road. At least he didn't charge for his fatal diagnosis.

She holds tight to Bluebird's hand, thumb in the direction of town. One helpful attribute of children is their lack of perspective, their sweet, dumb trust.

Dreadlocks, Hallie explains, looking over at their driver. Right? My daughter needs to know about your hair (which is like some torn up, bright orange sink scrubber on top of flat, trout-colored eyes).

Ya, guesso.

A musician. Had to be. They shunned speech as unrefined substance. Bluebird's father had been a drummer, hyper, mute.

Five dollars you're a musician?

Yeah but no five dollars.

Veering the Volkswagen, he hits the curb, pulling in front of a man in a limp terry-cloth hat and plaid shorts videotaping an adobe doorway, his wife fanning herself with a map in the overhang of J. C. Penney's.

Town.

Swell. Thanks.

Hallie feels reckless with her puny cash, uninterested in aiming for mature, retentive behavior. When Bluebird starts jump-pleading in front of a toy store, she says, ok ok, *one* toy so long as it's not that, indicating the five-foot chili pepper wind sock blowing from the store's *vigaed* porch.

Bluebird walks out wearing a tiara of paste diamonds, flicking a wand with glitter and geegaw, taking up the sidewalk with real hogginess, chin hiked, body stiff. Halts before a souvenir drugstore on the plaza; it has a soda fountain. Here, brandishes the wand severely. An enormous green-black gorilla hunkers like a city zoo at one end of the counter, a newspaper propped in his shaggy paws; Bluebird runs in and wedges up next to him.

Here, Moomers.

Hallie drinks coffee, while her daughter sets gluey mosaics of pancake in front of the slumped gorilla.

What if he's real, Moomers?

Oh, sure he is. I'm quite sure he parties every night with loads of other gorillas.

A man next to them deftly flips the gorilla a toast crust, winks at Bluebird, peers myopically at Hallie. His hair is in two, rag-woven braids, his face mildly pocked and fleshy, his black glasses taped in the corners. He says he's going over to the community pool, where there's free showers. She feels guided, pays both bills.

Bluebird pounces on a yellow Wuzzles suit in the lost and found, Hallie takes a plain black. The indoor pool is empty. They hike backwards down the chrome ladder into heavily chlorinated, wrist-hot water. Bluebird anchors her crown with two hands while Hallie knots the canvas straps of an orange life preserver on her daughter's chalky shoulderwings.

Jeez. He's got one leg. Vaughn's only got one leg.

Ssh, stop staring, Hallie whispers.

Do you swim every day?

No. His breasts shake, puffy, the nipples so female-pointy Hallie has this goofy urge to put her mouth down and suck. His glasses are missing, his hair is wet, black twigs to his waist.

Bluebird drifts face up in her orange vest, diamonds skidding light off the water. Hallie goes under, rising like a slow, white lumpfish. From the deep end, she watches Vaughn, one leg finning, two arms plugging, how he gets out pushing hard with his arms, jigging to a bench to rub at his stump, a man shining up a scarlet, squarish doorknob. She swims over to Bluebird, and they stand in the pool, watch Vaughn against the wall, moving into the dressing room.

Five dollars he's a war hero, Hallie says.

They take turns under the lukewarm shower, rubbing their

hair with pink gel from the Eurobath box on the tiled wall. Neither has bathed since leaving Cheyenne; Bluebird sits at Hallie's feet, by the drain, patting the stopped-up water and singing.

Vaughn is facedown on a beige plot of chemically dead lawn, pink hollyhocks spindling up around him. Hallie's pretty sure he's drunk, was drunk at breakfast.

They cross the street to a park where Kit Carson lies obtrusively buried in one corner. There are swings, a slide, brown donkeys, yellow ducks and pink pigs on great silver coils. She and Vaughn sit on a bench, passing a quart of red Gallo, stewmeat wine, Hallie calls it, watching Bluebird, her face a little, uppy sphere of brightness. Behind the bluish metal slide, Hallie sees a figure with black mangly hair high in a cottonwood tree, rolled into a thin blanket, a pale green cigar.

Vaughn, who's that?

Charlie. He lives in the park, hangs out in trees.

Does he think he's a bird?

No. Vaughn took the bottle. He is a bird.

A few minutes later, Vaughn climbs into an old truck with a friend and takes off. Bluebird has found a girl to play with, they crouch beneath the slide, building twig and stone houses. Hallie feels socketed to the bench, accumulating flaws as a mother. What's-his-name's still snagged in the tree, in his blanket, green, caught like a kite. There must be worse things people did than running off with their kids when things got bad, running out of money, transportation and hopeful ideas. She'd gotten pregnant way too soon, that was it. Too young.

They catch a ride back to the Pinch Penny. Hallie pays a dollar to get their tangled, wet stuff out of the back room, shoves everything into the dryer, which has modern blue digital seconds ticking, thumbs through a stack of Jehovah's Witness magazines, all there is to look at. Bluebird headlocks the dog to her belly, its legs sag listlessly.

So Hallie's got the grapefruit box of laundry sliding off her hip, walking hobbled into a fiesta pink sunset; she can barely make out the bulky figure hunched over the Impala's opened, white hood. Hoping for the dour, greedy mechanic, even when she's right up beside him, seeing exactly, inevitably, who it is.

He straightens, rubbing sly, clubby hands on a red rag.

Linkage, that's it. All that was wrong.

How'd you get here?

Oooh, who's overjoyed? He reaches down, squeezes Bluebird on one shoulder. Hiya sportfan. Bluebird slow-drills, undrills, one foot into nicked up cement ground.

Here. Gallantly hefting the laundry box from Hallie's hip, kneeing open the door of the Impala, setting the box on the torn seat.

Anybody hungry? I passed a place down the road, looks pretty decent.

Taking the wheel, taking over again, thinking silence is kin to forgiveness. Still, Hallie's thinking how Bluebird hasn't eaten since the drugstore breakfast.

The Pueblo Restaurant is fluorescent lit, oxblood Formica tables, turquoise plastic chairs, blobby green hearts of philodendron snaking across the ceiling. They sit by the mud fireplace, a metal fan on its ledge, a red and gold plaster Buddha, benign, incongruous, stuck where fire's supposed to go. Bluebird and Hallie drink Cokes out of gold, pebbled glasses while he goes to the rest room. The waitress brings two beers, Hallie pointing where to set them, where he's sitting.

Are you glad he found you, Moomers?

Hardly.

But I like being with you. Just with you.

I like that too. Ohgod, Bluey, it's hard sometimes.

What?

Life. You know. Deciding what's best.

By the time Rick is at the cash register, paying, his wide, primitive back to her, she wants to be lying down with him, under him, this feeling, unwanted, resisted, beats out her caution and her anger.

He walks back, staring into her eyes the whole way across the grainy, bright room, a toothpick jutting from his white teeth, grinning, unsubtle. Half the time he reads her thoughts.

There's apartments right next door, twenty-one bucks a night. I got us one.

How did you find us?

Don't matter. How I got here, how I knew where you'd run to this time. Don't matter in any long or short run. It don't matter so don't ask.

Bluebird comes over, begging one more quarter to put in the glass machine that cracks out hard, shiny candies in fruit shapes. It ate my first one, she pouts.

He hands her two quarters, the whole time staring at Hallie

like some cornball stunt he's absorbed from believing in movies.

Work's been good. I picked up an extra two hundred last week. That should help with the bills. And I replaced that pipe in the bathroom.

Waltzing her around. First waltz, then shove, that's his way. She ignores him, watching the cook behind the partition, fat, bland-cheeked, a chef's hat like a starched glacier on his head, polishing a frying pan, bringing it near his face, a woman with a hand mirror.

Rick swivels to check who she's seeing other than him. Damn I hate that, you looking at other men all the time.

I don't look at other men. I look at people.

Bullshit.

Bluebird comes back, bright pygmy bananas and oranges and limes clicking and rolling like the tropics on the black rabbit skin. She plops her head on Hallie's shoulder, yawning.

Ricky jogs, Bluebird on his shoulders, over to the apartment. Hallie holds two beers, one in either hand. When they get inside, Hallie sees two double beds, lifts Bluebird's crown off, kisses the ovaled heat of her head. Okay, Bluey, time to brush teeth and pee, get ready for bed.

When they come out of the bathroom, Rick's set up in his underwear in a plastic chair in front of the TV, the diamond crown tipped backwards, sliding off his big shaggy head. Bluebird shrieks, runs and jumps on his lap, thumb in mouth, hoping to stay up, watching TV on his lap.

Hallie's voice cuts in, nearly jealous.

Hey guys. Time for bed.

*

He won't kiss her, doesn't bother, just moves his fingers up her in a deliberate way that makes her bite her arm to keep quiet. Next moving his fingers out, teething and chewing a row of hickeys on her neck, stopping to say he loves screwing her. Only her.

Love is confusing, love is sickness, Hallie thinks, the body tearing off one way, the mind another. He reaches an arm down, picks up the beer, drinks. The TV stays on the whole time, no sound, while he's doing stuff to her, calmly glancing over at the TV, watch it, watch her, watch it. Want some? Holding the bottle above her head. No. She's wondering about Vaughn, his one leg, how would it be, him climbing on top of both her and Ricky, a weight, buffalo-weight, and how would his blank leg space feel. He might have been her friend. At dinner, Bluebird had told him about the gorilla, the Indian with one leg, and Rick had laughed. Yeah, your mom can reel in some weird trash.

And we saw this other man in the park who sits in trees and thinks he's a bird.

Fucking loony bird. Loony birds all over these days.

Hallie kicks him under the table. She hates for him to swear around her child.

Basement gray in the TV light, he's grabbing her butt, grinning at her, pinching it lightly, his eyes near-mean. So you're already out picking up Indians. Miss Wanna-Be.

Wanna-Be?

Wanna-Be-an Indian.

Right. Where does it go?

Where does what go? He belches.

All the sweat, you know, after we make love.

Huh. Into the air I guess. Evaporation.

Five bucks it falls back down as rain. Our sweat comes down on people, their sweat comes down on us.

You're pretty crazy, you know that? And you do always look at other guys.

To stop the tears from trickling into her scalp, to reverse their slide, Hallie props on her elbows, stares at the crown on top of the TV, street light giving it more false sparkles.

Calm was forming in her again, massive, fabricated, numbing. She walked into it like a picture, a picture of driving back to Cheyenne, the windows sealed up tight, the white Impala all sweetstinking like a high school dance. Ricky was going to buy that drugstore gorilla, he'd said that, falling asleep, and Hallie bet on how it would be, her and him in the backseat, down necking, Bluebird up front, peaceful as an adult in her diamond crown, switching radio stations, the gorilla taking charge, hands slow to react, dumb as any love, gigantic on the wheel.

The Erotic Life of Luther Burbank

[1]

Our life was one of complete happiness.
— EMMA L. BURBANK, July 1895
Santa Rosa, California

A feckless, long-armed girl named Maudie Dollar roamed the
trellised porch, her borrowed shoes pinching from a solid
week's compliance to the demands, however genteelly couched,
of Burbank's three women. Moving dreamily, with an occasional limp from her cramped, spotted shoes, she wanted
proof he was on his way, not keeping Dr. Baily dismally poised
over a cooling supper, not fatally late for his own (the grayed
shin of beef, the boiled, salted potato, the famous Early Rose
he had, at the age of twenty-four, coaxed from one miracle
spore, a ruddy-jacketed, creamy-fleshed potato that had so
spectacularly advanced his seedsman's reputation).

In time, Maudie loped into the green-striped dining room
to pronounce her employer arrived. She had observed him,
diminutive god of the vegetable kingdom, stooping along the
oyster shell path in his wilted black suit and high-crowned
straw hat, its narrow black band haloed with dirt from his ex-

perimental gardens. Emerging minister and spirit captain of his fruit trees and grapevines and roses, his rampant thousands of freak hybrids and reckless grafts, the green, easy profligacy of his seedlings, coming in as he always did, faded and spent, to a supper Maudie had slid with her speckled, rootlike arms before him, the food unimaginative but slightly, anyway, still warm.

The heavy green bottle of anise liqueur, Dr. Liberty Hyde Baily's gift, stood snubbed and unopened on the table with its damasked cloth the frail color of halved pear. The Dean of New York's Agricultural College had just been apprised of Mother Burbank's primmest and most public virtue. Her lips had not been near a drop of liquor in eighty-six years. Son Luther, and daughter, Emma, had likewise and with perhaps small choice in the matter, followed suit. Mother Burbank now sat with a dowager's remote complacency across from Dr. Baily while Emma Burbank, a specter in her paling forties, sat to his left. Of Luther's wife, Dr. Liberty Hyde Baily knew nothing save the drama of her absence. She was upstairs, insisting, apparently as always, she would not attend supper without her husband. This occasioned Maudie Dollar's next duty, one carried out with inventive spirit, hollering up the polished oak stairs that somebody's husband was on the porch this minute even as she yelled, his world-famous hand, a hand intimate with thousands of fertile plants, on the door handle.

"This resembles precisely a brain, don't you agree, Dr. Baily?" Helen Coleman Burbank had opened the anise liqueur with a greedy aptitude and now balanced half of a walnut meat on her paint-smeared fingertip near the candle flame. She had been upstairs all afternoon, touching up yet another miniature oil portrait of herself. "The question persists — is it an intelligent brain or the brain of an idiot?"

As she stubbed the nut into her opened mouth, chewing voluptuously, Helen stared at her mother-in-law and said, "What do you think, Mother Burbank?"

"I think it is one of the walnuts from Luther's trees, simply that, a walnut, either from the Paradox or the Royal."

Helen stuck out a nut-smeared tongue, drained off her liqueur, narrowed her suggestive gaze at their visitor. "It was the brain of an idiot. In fact, I feel the stupider for having eaten it. Dr. Baily, do not eat a single one of these nuts, they will rob you of your considerable intelligence, an aspect seductive in any man. Luther, what did you do all day? Potter about in your weeds with your little battery of camel hair brushes? Breeding this with that? Your face is mottled with passion, remarkably like a map I once saw of the West Indies."

Olive Burbank leaned toward her son, brushing his thin hair, the color of grayed ivory, off his forehead while Luther continued implacably chewing, his gaze fixed on the flayed jacket of his dinner potato. He seemed neither to hear his wife's pettish voice nor to feel the doting tyranny of his mother's hand.

"My son, Dr. Baily, gave another of his garden tours this afternoon, his fourth this week. Hundreds of pilgrims besides yourself arrive on our property to see evidence of Luther's exceptional genius with plants. He is besieged, as anyone can see from the mountain of correspondence in the corner, letters from all the nooks and crannies of the globe. A reserved man, my son nevertheless commands the world, modestly and without complaint."

"The Plant Wizard they call him," Helen went on, playing with the humpy shells of her walnuts, clicking them conjugally together.

"Maudie, bring us two coffees please." Mother Burbank ignored her daughter-in-law as she had done with mounting tenacity since the campaign to prevent her son's union with this Jezebel had failed. "Mr. Burbank is past his endurance, and Dr. Baily, who has traveled all this way from New York, must be exhausted as well."

"If Luther is tired, I can well speak for my husband," Helen said oversweetly. A woman maligned and unceasingly gossiped over in this rural town, Helen Coleman Burbank had been condemned as an adventuress of calculated design who, it was most recently rumored, had blacked both her husband's eyes after pointing a loaded rifle at him. Such tattle swarmed with gnatlike obstinance, and Helen Burbank treated both rumor and fact impartially, as pests, bothersome but easily swatted off.

"I can speak with both assurance and authority for my husband. I will even speak of that which he cannot, of that which is more certainly the truth about him."

Emma scraped back her chair. "I won't stand for this."

"You just did," Helen observed coolly. "Dr. Baily, my husband loves children in the extreme. He would like one of his own yet his capacity to generate a child is dim indeed.

"My husband" — and so saying, Helen Burbank flicked at one of the unbroken walnuts so it tumbled modestly in Luther's direction and dropped off the table edge — "it is challenging, is it not, to pollinate one's wife from the distance of a dismal cot above the barn, where you have slept now for the past two years? My justification for chasing off those whey-faced neighbor's children you invite onto our property, those humiliating phantom children, is to leave considerable latitude for you, dearest, to cross the lawn, come up to our bed and get a child of your own."

Emma fled upstairs, slamming all the doors, again and again, creating, as was her wont, Dr. Baily was told, a kind of thunderous sensation above their heads.

Unperturbed, Maudie Dollar slid a cup of strong coffee under Mr. Burbank's nose. As always, he appeared oblivious to this overheated mares' nest. Dr. Baily, on the other hand, wore a refined expression of shock tempered by the guilty pleasure of witnessing unpredicted domestic tumult. Maudie Dollar was immune — such squallings and tempests were common-place, resistant to formal prayer and her own occasional threats to quit.

There ensued a prolonged interval of silence before the Plant Wizard spoke, his voice reedy and compelling, gender-less. "The Satsuma graft has taken. This morning I bit into so many of the plums on the different shoots, I have gotten quite a sour stomach."

[11]

"I love everybody! I love everything! All things — plants, animals and men — are already in eternity traveling across the face of time, whence we know not, whither who is able to say.

*Do you think Christ or Mohammed, Confucius, Baal or even
the gods of ancient mythology are dead? Not so. Do you think
Pericles, Marcus Aurelius, Moses, Shakespeare, Spinoza, Aristo-
tle, Tolstoi, Franklin, Emerson are dead? No. For the little soul
that cries aloud for continued personal existence for itself and its
beloved there is no help. For the soul which knows itself no more
as a unit, but as a part of the universal unity of which the
beloved is also a part — for that soul there is no death."*

— from a speech given by LUTHER BURBANK at the
First Congregational Church, San Francisco, 1925

"What man can explain why he lives, Dr. Baily?" Luther
Burbank waved his hand to indicate the whole preposterously
fruited, dusky blue orchard in which they sat. Neither could
help regarding the figure of Emma, clad in a Hellenic sort of
tunic, flittering up and down the immaculate rows, erratic as a
moth and mainly ungraceful, though hypnotic due to her constancy of motion and subtle variation. Liberty Hyde Baily had
noted through the entirety of his dinner (a poky dish served in
a volatile atmosphere, really, he would have preferred the reverse), how remarkably like her brother she was, deliberately
so, as though he were some Ideal Pattern and her ambition to
tailor herself to it. How devoted her behavior on his behalf,
acting more the servant than the servant. She had even risen
from her chair at one point, leaned across the table to reposi-
tion the limp napkin about his neck, a thing he submitted to
docilely, a tribute absorbed without fuss. One could, Baily
mused, and to some degree found himself titillated by such a
notion, mistake the sister for the wife.

It was here, during the halfway point in his interview, Dr.
Baily discovered himself in the discomfiting posture of inter-

viewer turned confidant. Did the recent death of his own wife award him such mortal melancholy as to prompt the small, almost child-figured man beside him to unburden himself? To Dr. Baily's knowledge, the man beside him was a nearly mythic American hero, messianic in his claims and concept of himself — a Darwinist given over to hyperbolic conceits, scorned by botanists as something of a fraud, a man who, beginning with that enigmatical root, the potato, revived Eden on earth, promising a hybridized paradise in every backyard, purchasable through seed catalogs. This is what Baily knew. Even now, in the gold- and violet-striped dusk, they sat among tapestried rows of trees bearing neither one fruit nor the other. Dozens of varieties of fruits weighed jubilant from every tree, a potently fragranced labyrinth of grafting . . . a sexual hodgepodge, and what was rejected, what would not succeed, would be, at Luther Burbank's command, destroyed. The sight of one hundred bonfires flaring colossally along the fenced perimeters of this world-famous experimental nursery was not uncommon. A demigod's refuse.

And now Liberty Baily understood something else, a thing which would lend a grace note of sympathy to a certain widely read article he would publish. Luther Burbank, national icon, spiritually vain horticulturalist, could not tend to his own wife.

"How did you meet?" Baily asked because, frankly, he wondered.

"I had just spoken at the Fitchfield Fair in my hometown of Lunenburg, Massachusetts, and was taking the train back to Santa Rosa. A young widow from Denver sat beside me. I found myself, under her persistent examination, uncovering my dreams, philosophies, desires. I have since learned that dangerous women obscure their motives. Dr. Baily, I confess to you with the easy anguish of hindsight, Helen only wished to dig out of me how much of a fortune I had. The woman totted up the promising sums of myself, then coldly, with mathematical precision, set about procuring me. This is what I have come to believe, and it has greatly discouraged me."

"Did you care for her?"

"Dr. Baily, I have 'loved,' as you say, twice, and both times been unseated. In the case of Helen, I married with the intent of no longer being a burden to either my sister or my mother, both of whom have taken care of me all my life. I had thought to attempt a family of my own. Now Helen keeps herself upstairs, painting, reading a great deal, sharpening her malice on the whetstone of books. She has become vindictive. I tell you, a man who has given over the whole of his life to the contemplation of and experimentation with fertile generations of plants cannot hope to triumph over the fickle and constant violations of the human heart. I am, in this thing, dismally failed."

Neither of them heard, but just then Emma floated behind her brother and, clapping her frail hands over his eyes, murmured in his ear. For a second time that evening, Liberty Baily had the troubling and distinct sense of being witness to something, to the suggestion that these two were sweethearts, chastely and filially bound. Observing this brother and sister in their darkening, byzantine orchard, he felt an awkward sympathy for Burbank's wife (news of their bitter divorce would not much surprise him, nor would a subsequent letter from Burbank himself, nearly incoherent in its condemnation of his mother and his sister as the triumphant agents of his marital failure). What part but that of termagant remained for a wife in this house? She could not rival the fanatic devotion of the sister or challenge maternal sovereignty. It seemed to Baily that like bonfires flaring fitfully along the edges of this property, three women burned, endlessly, inextinguishably, inside one man's house. Did their sacrifice, a theater unobserved, amend the bright business of creation? Indifferent to what tribulation he left in his breeder's wake, Luther Burbank, it seemed to Dr. Baily, was a clever, unperturbed man. Distracted by their wretched quarreling, the women overlooked its subject, leaving their little horticulturalist quite amiably alone.

Years later, Baily would describe the impression made on him that July evening, seated in the Plant Wizard's field of oddities, an impression fading quickly, an ornate dream one is relieved, upon waking, to abandon.

[III]

On the Occult Nature of My Sexual Proclivities
— L.B.

They are out of their Sunday best, of course, Maudie and Eugene, raveling like thick ginger roots in the fallow heat, their skin pale and damp as vinegar.

(I speak frankly now, safely settled, concealed behind the wall and its gap fashioned by me from which to regard with one straining eye, the coupling of healthy and vigorous stock. The male scion a brilliant and weekly insertion into the bluish cleft, so like an old-fashioned Josephine rose, a primal, imperiled mouth. I hold my own dwarfish scion in my hands, feel its tumid impulse, its wish to claim the narrow aperture and so grow wise.)

"Look." Maudie sets Eugene's work-swollen hand over her wide, dappled throat, on the goiter disfiguring its cool base. "It's better now. Last evening he held his hand over it, and I saw a raining of light behind my eyes, and my throat grew hot and congested. Eugene, it feels fine now when I swallow."

"But Maudie, sweet."

"What? What's wrong?"

"Feel." He takes her hand. "An awful swelling here. It's just happened. Do you think your old Mr. Burbank can heal that?"

She flops on him, thrashing like a hooked fish, chewing on his ear till he yelps.

"Shh. Someone might hear."

Then Maudie's long back, familiar to me now, speckled as a trout lily's, halves the only light in the room.

(This is most potent breeding, a curative stimulant to myself, so anxious in my own infrequent coupling, a compensatory bliss by which I am timidly appeased. My modest size has advantage, I can fit myself cannily into the smallest portion of nonthreatening space.)

"I've got to go." Maudie tosses on a hurly-burly of clothes, sloppily replaiting her coppery hair. Eugene, his hands clasped behind his head, watches.

She bends to lace her borrowed shoes. "He's not like anybody else. There's no way to account for a person like that, he's placed apart by destiny, that's what I've come to think, Eugene."

"Well, just so the healer's hands keep to your throat and that's all of it, dear Maudie."

[IV]

Paramahansa Yogananda Walks with Luther Burbank

Paramahansa Yogananda has the eyes, Maudie thinks, as she serves their spiritualist visitor hot peppermint tea, of a cow, humid and infinitely kind. When he looks at her, she feels a heavenly nostalgia pass over her heart, beyond any naked sweetness she has felt with Eugene. She will feel this each time he visits, each of the six times he walks with Luther through the bee-clamoring, convoluted gardens, his virginal silk turban like an exotic milky bloom, like another of Luther Burbank's botanical wonders. She serves him, the tray light on her gravid belly, on the seeded child, as Yogananda talks freely of mystic conjunctions between the raising of plants and of humans, of the vibrations and powers of divine love. Love is discussed a great deal, its powers beyond romance or fertility, it is the love Maudie has heard in Luther Burbank's voice as he talks to each of his plants, inviting them never to be afraid. Training, breeding, selection, vibration of spirit, love, the conversation between them both simple and arcane. And Luther, as ever, in his one drab unseasonable suit, his black vest and starched shirt, determinedly unacquainted with his own body, its concealed workings, its organic decline into first betrayal, then release.

[v]

How to Judge Vegetable Novelties

In March of 1920 there was a parade. Luther had previously confided to a Dr. D. B. Anderson, his dentist, that there were said to be thirteen Christs and most probably he, Luther, was one. The parade did not acknowledge this but, still, it was a festival and birthday pageant for the great artificial pollinator, the great mother of the Burbank potato, the stoneless prune, the walnut, the spineless cactus (debacle or no), the Shasta daisy, the Paul Bunyan rhubarb and the chimerical blue rose. The vegetable promiscuity of the man continued to astonish the world, especially the women of Santa Rosa, the women of all the church groups and temperance leagues of America. Luther Burbank walked all his life on a leash of women, his hands never still, moving from plant to plant, spreading yellow pollen, he loves me he loves me not he loves me he loves me not the incessant hum that followed him all his green and provocatively fertile life. Improving over eight hundred fruits and flowers in fifty years, burning hundreds of thousands of hybrid seedlings, berry bushes, stock trees grafted with dozens of different hybrid fruits, in bonfires like the white volatile flarings of creation itself. He abetted the sexuality of plants, profligate in his erotic urge to perfection.

> All hail to Luther Burbank
> The wizard of the flowers
> They know your magic wand
> In your own native country

And ev'ry foreign land
All hail to Luther Burbank, all hail!
— Composed for the birthday parade by
the egregious ADA KYLE LYNCH

Costumed as flowers and fruits, as buds and blossoms, the children assembled for the "Burbank March," moving down the clay-hard streets of Santa Rosa, singing "All Hail." Four children, two boys and two girls, each outfitted as a rose, were selected to read Luther Burbank's life story. As they stepped forward to sing "Birthday Song," two other children, a pear and a peach blossom, hoisted an unwieldy banner with a picture of Mr. B. at its center, bordered with an oversize red, frilly heart. Painted above the heart in plump green letters, the year of the Plant Wizard's birth. The pageant lasted exactly an hour and concluded with a strange Yell.

The children's beloved Santa Rosa seedsman would die, hiccoughing, in his bed during April, the cruelest month, 1926. Emma, with Maudie Dollar's help, would carry out his wish to be buried under a cedar of Lebanon near the house. He was seventy-seven years old, his Beloved Emma seventy-two.

[VI]

Self-Fertilization in the Vegetable Kingdom
— L.B.
after death,
speaks

I embarked, when I was fifteen, on what was called in those days the "water cure," a kind of health fad. Each night I carried a heavy pail of water upstairs to my bedroom. By morning it would be frozen over, and I was obliged to break the ice with a stick of firewood. With this water, I would sponge bathe. During the time of this water cure, many times, I left open my window and snow drifted over my bed as I slept. I ate no meat and very little other food, rejoicing in this ardent regime until I was invincible, until my parents forbade me to go on with it, concerned as to my wasted physical being and diminished strength. Mortification of the flesh, they named it, and I, mocked by hunger, for such was my desire, agreed.

Declared as dead now, our flesh breaking casually into potent soil, Mother and I wait for our daughter and our sister, watch with proud, pale amusement as she whittles her solitary days and nights around our old home, composing a somewhat cluttered and sentimental book about me, beginning with the line "Our life was one of complete happiness." *Oh false sister!* Our life was one of suppressed longing covered over by spirit adulation and psychic preoccupation, the lush choirings of garden.

We are not visible to Emma. I do not manifest as Mother did to me after her death, standing each night by the foot of my bed, haranguing me — my health, my health, my health, they are praying for you, Luther, the women of this world, they worry you do not believe in God, they hear the word *infidel* and pray the harder and with misguided fervor. Tell them, Luther, you are God, you are Napoleon if you like, you are immortal, Son! Can anyone blame me? I would distract myself from the terrifying monotony of those nightly speeches by seeing what a dead person such as my mother might wear. Judging by what was half-glimpsed and half-imagined, some sort of

plain pleated urnlike gown of a mauve luster, with a garland-
ing of darkest green myrtle such as the Greeks wore, encircling
her large, classically proportioned head. I tell you it is a reliev-
ing and timeless thing, to wait for my sister. We fertilize ourselves after all, from pollen that drifts like snow everywhere,
the invisible, atomic architecture of all. I wait inside Mother's
humid and pervasive green dominion, for my Beloved, who
waited for me when as a boy I would return cold and dirty
from a day's excursion into the eastern woodlands. I stand at
the edge of this world and will take her hand when the time
comes. Here there is no barrier to obtaining fruits of any size,
form or flavor desired, none to producing plants and flowers
of any form, color or fragrance; all that is needed is knowledge
to guide our efforts, undeviating patience and a cultivated eye.

Of late, Emma has taken to wandering our bare, wintry orchard, sleepless and cold, her ice-thin hair fluttering, intent on
searching among wet and dormant branches for someone hud-
dled here, ripely hers.

Climb higher, sister, hook your arches around the dama-
scened bark of this tree I once forged in tribute to your perfection, a bold and holy grafting, provision for rebirth, good
breeding observed. Accept my hand, cool and formless as it is,
into God's Paradise, that empyreal, wet but flaring region
where all seeding, all manner of love's offspring, even we, Darling One, are allowed, are welcomed and overwatched, belong-
ing, neither high nor low, to that vast parade of Cherished and
Celestial Stock.

The Instinct for Bliss

Frances Waythorn, her face soured and ghastly as a mime's from a cosmetic paste of yogurt, scrubs walls and wainscoting, praying for bleach, polish, order, something, to check her daughter's latest slide from innocence. Pockets the Bic lighter, so Athena can't smoke. Weasels under the bed, dredging out a feculent nest of candy wrappers, cigarette butts, lewd notes, blood-soiled underwear, so Athena won't get fat or have sex or die. Frances's motions are selfless and efficient, her behavior a worship extending into grief. She refuses to acknowledge the poster of Jim Morrison. If she follows her own heat, stripping his deviant's baby face off the wall above her daughter's bed, who knows what might happen. Mothers like Frances are no longer immune from the retaliation of their daughters. Her face beginning to itch under the dried yogurt, Frances swivels a plush bunny into the center of the eyelet-edged pillow. Her child's room is pulled back, once again, into an immaculate relief of white, except for the poster, unexpungeable as a stain.

Athena, legally halved, is batted lightly between her parents. On alternate weeks she is not at her father's, she resides with Frances, her white room declining into a dank, fetid emporium of sloth. Those Sunday afternoons when Athena arrives, a canny refugee, on her mother's doorstep, a soiled, lumpy pillowcase of belongings over one shoulder, declaring she is an atheist who has drunk the blood of stray cats, Frances's labor, much like that of Sisyphus, begins anew, no hope for reprieve, only the diligent loosening of familiar, defiant knots.

Frances is, in fact, uncrumpling and reading, rereading Athena's smutty notes before packing for her drive to a Navajo wool workshop, when the doorbell rings. Hollering "Wait," then "Sorry," unlocking the door, her face dripping water and patchy, as if with plaster, she sees he has a lovely, surprisingly tender face, this Officer Ruiz, telling her Athena is at the police station with another girl, arrested for shoplifting. He has been busy, attempting to notify the girls' parents. (Guiltily, Frances remembers three distinct times the phone rang as she scavenged under Athena's bed.)

"Where in God's name is her father? She's staying with him this week."

"Ma'am, from what your daughter claims, Mr. Waythorn is in Albuquerque until tomorrow."

He then informs Frances she can come get Athena or agree to her being held overnight in juvenile detention.

"Of course I'll get her, though I am about to leave for Arizona. What about the other girl?" Frances asks, not really caring, angry that once again, and predictably, Athena's father has left her in the dark, told her nothing of his plans, neglected his daughter and spoiled her own small hope for independence.

"Her parents have requested she be held overnight."

"In the Taos jail? Good lord. At their age I was in a convent. Reciting Shakespeare. Doing as I was told. Though Athena's father was a delinquent, a truant, he's boasted that often enough."

Frances's tone is bitter, as if she had known him even then, as if she had been harmed, even then, by her husband's arrant boyhood.

So far, Frances decides, this driving across the hammered-flat desert is largely a matter of virulent silence.

Athena catches at a shifting avalanche of cassettes falling from her lap.

"May I play the Red Hot Chili Peppers? Their lyrics are banned." With Frances, almost any "Mother May I?" works.

"Banned?" Frances attends carefully, thinks she identifies the phrase *donkey juice* shouted over and over.

"I can't clearly make them out, honey. The words."

Pleased, Athena spritzes her face and arms with water from the plastic spray bottle she's brought, fogging herself like some fragile, costly plant.

"Want some?"

Tepid mist hits Frances, wetting her face. She has a pale rash from the yogurt.

Right now she would rather feed than punish Athena, pad her with double cheeseburgers, damp fries, chocolate shakes. If she's fat, no boy will want to have sex with her. If she's fat, she might not steal. Possibly no one but her mother will want her. She casts a look at Athena, the combat boots, unpolished and heavy looking as bricks, shredded jeans, black tank top, the front of her hair in two taffetalike maroon flaps, the back of her head a shaved greenish stubble. The starlike design inked onto her upper arm, Frances is afraid to ask if it is a satanic emblem or simply the declaration of an atheist. What if Athena belongs to a cult, a gang? Frances remembers the heavyset woman in a purple tunic on Oprah Winfrey, sobbing, saying you never, ever, know what your children do once they leave the house, you think you do, but you don't. Her son had been machine-gunned outside the front door. Actually, it is Frances whose stomach is bloating, whose thighs have widened.

"Ma-Maah." Athena says it like a doll. "Where are you heisting me?"

"To a workshop on dyeing wool. I signed up for it at an arts fair last month, a freak impulse because I've never woven or dyed a thing in my life. But, Athena, at my age, let me tell you, inventing a new life is no zip-i-dee-doo-dah flick of the wrist."

"May I drive?"

"No."

"Pleeze, Ma-Mah? Dad lets me drive his truck sometimes."

"Absolutely not. You're supposed to be in jail. And your father's decisions, as you well know, are never mine. Look how he's abandoned you."

"He lets me do what I want, that's different. It is grotesque out here, Ma-Maaah."

"Really? I think it has its own beauty. Deserts are spiritual places. Points of transcendence."

This observation rebounds, stilted. And why is Athena talking to her like a rubber doll?

"A couple of things we're to remember when we get there. Can you lower that a bit?"

Athena blunts, reluctantly, her music.

"When you're introduced, you're not to look any of the Navajos directly in the eye."

"Why not?"

"They consider it overly intimate."

"Cool."

Frances glances over. She never knows what will be cool or why.

"A simple enough thing for you."

"What?"

"You never look me in the eye, Athena. Not anymore."

"Not." She pins her mother with a look startlingly lethal. "Is that genuine? That's frightening."

Athena shrugs. "What was the other thing? You said there were two."

"Fish. You can't eat fish around them. Navajos believe fish are embryonic, unformed humans, something like that. I can't remember. It's in here" — Frances pats the guidebook on Navajo culture she has brought, largely unread.

"Fish sticks make me puke anyways."

"Anyway."

"Any-waaaays. . . ."

With the toe of her boot, Athena turns up the banned, incoherent lyrics.

What finally wakes her, after the others are up, is a sullen drone of flies along the heat-warped window ledge. In a white plastic bucket, blacking the surface of their drinking water, is an uneven rug of drowned flies. A single fly still walks, if walking, she wonders, is how to describe it, along the battered lip of a tin cup. Frances rolls her sleeping bag next to Athena's, against one of the eight cinder-block walls of the hogan. She hasn't the least idea how to function in a Native American environment, but neatness is never an error. Manners are the same the world over, to quote her mother, and politeness, not sex, the true mortar of civilization. Frances's resolve, now that she is divorced against her will, is to "follow her bliss," a phrase she'd recently heard at a Wild Women of the West seminar, where one of the most astonishing things she had participated in was humping the earth to release pent-up male energy. This is why she has driven all the way out here, to a Navajo reservation. On instinct for bliss. She hasn't the least experience with dyeing wool or weaving anything. She can't even sew. What attracted her was being told this would be a place where, temporarily, no men were allowed.

Scraping open the wood door, Frances sees her red car parked under the yard light, haughtily disassociated from the three trucks, two of which have I ♥ SHEEP stickers on their bumpers while her car has a blue sticker, stuck there by Athena, an upside-down cow on it saying MEAT IS DEAD. Athena had left the window on her side down, and with the car so close to the hogan, Frances sees a ratty-tailed, saffron rooster patrolling the front seat, back and forth, back and forth, its flat eye proprietary and arrogant.

"Hey Ma-mah, coffee."

Athena holds out a green, chipped mug; she's wearing yesterday's clothes, her mouth smeared a pinkish mahogany, a beauty dot penciled above the bow of her top lip. Over

Athena's bare shoulder, if she squinches up her eyes, Frances can make out a half circle of Navajo women bent over an animal of some sort, trussed and quivering on its back.

"Ma-Mah, poke on your glasses. You need to see this. They're going to kill a sheep."

Before leaving the hogan, neatly dressed in ironed jeans and a white-fringed, turquoise sweatshirt, Frances, her eyeglasses on, hesitates before a Navajo loom, its cotton warp a pale and tranquil lyre rising up from the muted, traditional design. Cocoons of wrapped yarn hang neatly along the rug's perfect edge, where the weaver stopped. Reluctant to go outside, Frances traces the design's black fretwork with one slowed finger, out to its edge.

She drinks her coffee, sitting on the ground beside a small cedar fire that burns with tallowy, weak effect in the morning sunlight. The grandmother squats behind the animal's throat, in a wide, pink-fanning skirt, red argyle socks and tennis shoes, her skirt the same medicinal pink as the outhouse, angled downhill as if it might tumble any time, exposing whoever sits, misfortunate, inside. Athena stands near the workshop instructor, a young Navajo woman named Valencia, who brushes a cedar branch, in blessing, over the animal. The grandmother, a white kerchief splashed with red roses concealing most of her face, pulls hard on its head, twists it, breaking the neck, then saws her long knife like a resined bow so blood sprays then spills with a green rushing of spring into a low white bowl, and the animal's bowels loose a sheen of dung onto the flat, colorless ground.

The fleece is split into a kind of jacket, its creamy lining veined with rich coral. The carcass still cinched within its parchment membrane, legs splayed four airy directions, suggests to Frances, except for the knob of breast, an upside-down table, fit to work on. The head, facing Frances, is set down in the fire. One eye swells, a black, glazed plum, the other sears and spits shut. The yellow wool blackens, crisps, stinks. Now the spirit of the animal is released from all boundary is everywhere.

This placid slaughter consoles Frances. A useful dismemberment, ritualized and strangely clean. The carcass squarely hung by hind feet from a cedar pole near the outdoor kitchen, the parchment membrane flensed back, the pursy insides unlocked, emptied out. The wine brown brooch of liver, for Frances goes to touch it, like warm sea glass. The taupe-gray skeins of intestine are pulled and stretched, the Navajo women pour hot water through the lengthened guts from an old tin coffeepot, squeezing and dribbling out the dung colored stuff. A ripe jeweling of ruby and pewter, pearled matter, a supple kingdom falling over the plain hard canvas of dirt, the dull, droughted, troubled-seeming earth spotted with blood like vital specklings of rain. The stomach with its sallow chenille lining, the drying gloss of lungs, liver, kidneys, draped over a narrow pole. And rising under the callus of blood in the milky flat-faced dish, like a mineral pool, strings of bubbles, a languorous spitting of bubbles, as if something deep under its weight still breathed.

Frances studies these women, the practical details of their butchering, their reverent pulling apart of a life and making it into other, smaller, useful things.

*

Two emergency room nurses from Lubbock are the only other participants in this workshop, and Frances has made no effort to talk to either one of them. A Married Rule, that pretense of sociability. The nurses, both skinny, both earnest and, for some reason, wan looking, stick close to the Navajo women, speak in enthusiastic twangings. Frances prays she doesn't resemble them, though she has signed up and paid for this experience, is conscious of being that evil necessity, a tourist with money to purchase a 3-D postcard, Navajo Women at Work on the Reservation. She wants to tell these Indian women she understands, but what is it she understands, and does she?

"Maa, Maaah . . . ."

Bleating, Athena shuffles outside the tilting outhouse, her nose pinched shut.

"You realize there are no males here. None. Except the sheep, and we've just killed him. When we eat him, he'll be gone, too."

"Oh, there are men." Frances's voice is muffled, weary. "Always and eternally there are men." She steps out of the terrible-smelling pink box. "My intent, Athena, was to go somewhere where, for once, there weren't any. And where the Navajo men who usually live here have gone, I can't imagine. I'm sure it's rude to ask."

They walk back down the slope, Frances whacking at her dusty pants. White pants. What had she been thinking?

"I need some smokes. I have to go into town."

"Town. For heaven's sake, Athena. Look where we are."

"Well, a trading post then. Plus I gotta wash my hair, it's

getting completely gross. There's a bathroom in their house, I went in and found it, but no water. You turn the faucets and air spits out. There's not even water in the toilet."

"There's a bad drought. I heard Valencia saying it's got something to do with the strip mining, with slurry water the mines use. All month they've been hauling water from town."

"These people should move to where there's more trees, more water. God." Athena narrows her eyes over the arid, hopeless, scrabbly landscape, blowing mournful smoke from her last cigarette. "Look. That dumb chicken's still on your front seat."

Athena runs, arms flapping, cigarette dangling, to swat the rooster out of the car. The Navajo women stop what they're doing to look, and Frances cannot interpret their faces. She jogs to catch up. She had looked forward to this trip by herself. She had hoped to learn something, or at least stop thinking about what exhausts and obsesses her. Now, looking into Athena's bright, provocative face, Frances sees how precisely, like a scissor cut, it matches her own at that age.

"Athena. You have to behave yourself. When you're the guest of another culture, you blend in, you ask intelligent questions."

"I am. I'm going to ask where the nearest store is and where the men are stashed."

"Athena."

"What."

"Please."

"What."

"You could be in prison right now. I could have left you there until your father decided to come and get you."

"Yada yada yada."

"What were you stealing?"

"Undies."

"Underwear? I just bought you plenty of — "

"Sexy underwear, Ma. You've never bought me that."

"May I ask you a simple question? What makes you so sure you are Jim Morrison's wife reincarnated?"

"You're the one who told me about reincarnation."

"Yes, but you can't just make up who you wish you had been. Oh, wouldn't I love to think I was once Thomas Jefferson or Sarah Bernhardt or even Beatrix Potter."

"Thomas Jefferson?"

"I've always wanted to be Thomas Jefferson. Do you know who I was in love with at your age?"

"Dad?"

Frances pauses dramatically. "Carl Sandburg."

"Who's that?"

"He's dead now, but he was a famous poet. I wrote Carl Sandburg several passionate letters. He was in his seventies."

"Cool. Mom in love with an old dude."

"I never mailed them. I knew he had a wife and a goat farm in North Carolina and probably he was happy."

"What about Dad? Oh, never mind. You'll just say something nasty. You're in that stage now."

"Stage?"

"Of divorce. Denial, rage, stuff like that."

"Where'd you pick up that idea?"

"Dad. He has books on divorce. Just like you."

"The same books?"

"Yup. Exactly. You guys are exactly alike."

Right, Frances thinks. Except he's chosen someone else. He's betrayed me.

Doing as she is asked, Athena drags the charred head from the fire by one gristled ear, sets it on a wood block, scrapes off filings of ash with a stick so the head can be wrapped and baked. And when she is certain her mother sees, for isn't her mother always watching, spying, jealous, easy to fool, a cinch to scare, so give her something to really be wigged about, Athena swoops one finger across the bowl of dulling blood and drives it deep into her own mouth. Not long after that, Frances will stand in the parrot yellow kitchen, stuffing gray, salted mutton into her mouth until the women, laughing, caution her to stop, until they stop laughing and take the plate away, saying this will make her sick. Mutton hunger is what they will say she has.

After lunch, they ride in the nurses' truck to the base of a sort of mountain. Everybody gets a plastic grocery sack. They are to follow the grandmother, collect twigs, leaves, roots and mosses, plants Valencia names for them, mullein, lichen, sumac, mountain mahogany, chamiso.

Athena lags behind with the more tired looking nurse, while Frances tracks the grandmother, what she can of her, two red argyled ankles flashing up a rigorous incline. Frances slows from the midday heat, the altitude, the enervating whiteness of the sun. In every direction, sealike troughs of land push up clumps of piñon and cedar, like rich, bronze-green kelp. A hawk skates the air above her in fluid, mahogany curls.

Frances nearly trips over the grandmother, crouched by a blunt formation of black rock, on her knees with a table knife, chipping chrome yellow powder from the rock and dusting it off her hands into a plastic bag.

Valencia looks up kindly. "We use this to get our black, mixing it with piñon pitch and cedar ash. It's pretty hard to find, but Grandmother is amazing, she goes right to where it is."

The taller nurse stands like a sentinel, a lank poplar, behind Frances.

"That stuff looks like uranium. Exactly."

Frances takes her turn scraping, grazing her knuckles; the uranium idea has unnerved her.

"You could hike up here once a year, get a gigantic load of this stuff to last you."

Frances thinks no one has heard, though the nurse's voice is tactless enough. The grandmother is resting in the compressed, thick shade of a piñon tree, while Valencia, wiping sweat from her forehead, answers, a perceptible teacher's edge to her voice.

"We take only what is needed each time. And Grandmother has taught us to leave an offering, a gift, before separating anything from where it is found."

"Halllooooo!" Athena, her arms making rapid pinwheeling motions, appears to be urging them up to the next highest ledge. Frances is busy, spit-washing a smudge of uranium off her turquoise shirt.

When the three white women attain the highest ledge, they hold their plastic bags of roots and twigs, panting, confounded by what they see. Inches deep across the ground lay thousands of pottery shards. The women, winded, hot-faced, are told they are standing on a trash dump, where Anasazi Indians, centuries ago, had thrown their broken pots and garbage.

The Navajo women sit and rest, observe the three white women stooping and bobbing, pecking about for bits of clay, their arms blooming with what they cannot seem to gather up fast enough. At first, the women call back and forth excitedly, then lapse into quiet, the weight of anthropology, the burden of choosing among priceless relics falling almost gloomily upon them. Like children, their greed eventually tires them, and they become aware of the Navajo women, quietly watching. They stop, arms and pockets and bags loaded down, their small congress embarrassed, bits of pottery dropping off them like leaves.

"Perhaps just two or three," says one nurse.

"Those that mean the most," suggests the other.

As Frances sets down her cumbersome pile, Athena, who had wandered off, returns. Between her hands, rests a large, perfect potshard, a black lightning streak down its reddish, curved flank. Exclaiming over its size and near-perfect condition, Frances begins to thank Athena, grateful for the largeness of gesture, the love implied.

"It's for Dad," Athena says softly. "I wanted to bring him something."

"Oh." Frances drops to her knees, shuffling through her little clay bits, as if to choose.

"Did you leave an offering?"

"Yuppers. My last cigarette, one I copped from the nurse."

On the ride back, they stop beside a faded sprawl of prickly

pear to pick its mushy, red fruits for pink dye. The driving
nurse, feeling unwell, decides to drive to the trading post for
stomach medicine. Both nurses drop the women back at the
hogan except for Athena, who's begged a ride.

Frances labors alongside her instructor, hefting enamelware
kettles and a halved oil drum filled with hauled water, onto
different fires. She sorts through gathered plant materials, carries bags and baskets of hand-spun wool skeins out from the
hogan, admires Valencia's long, black hair, twisted in a shining
bundle at the nape of her neck, noting its resemblance to the
skeins of wool, to the little bundles of yarn dangling from the
edge of the rug inside the hogan. She wonders how Valencia
would raise a daughter, how do the women raise teenagers out
here, how, in her own case, could things get much worse.

Swirling the stained waters with an ashy stick, made sleepy
by the steam of plants, bitter or sweet smelling, or dense as
soured earth, Frances begins to hope Athena might not return
until much, much later.

At once she hears the truck, observes it dipping and rising
over the rutted gullies, with Athena, cross-legged in the bed of
the truck, in a somber corona of dust, brandishing a cigarette.
As her daughter trips unsteadily past her, blowing smoke out
both nostrils, her maroon hair tangled and shreddy-looking,
Frances studies the shaven back of her head so disturbingly in-
fantlike, watches her wobble around a cast-iron pot of chamiso
dye, right herself, then pitch behind one side of the hogan and
begin, audibly, to vomit.

One of the nurses comes up to Frances.

"I found this in the truck bed."

Frances stares at the half-empty bottle.

The bottle lodged under her arm, Frances uses a peeled stick to raise out of the water one of the skeins of yarn. It hangs from the end of the willow stick, a twist, an eight, of deep, ardent gold.

Worse than finding Athena on the ground, is seeing the rooster, pecking with cold disregard, at her daughter's vomit. Frances is about to kick the rooster, when suddenly, admitting nature's genius, she leaves it to clean the mess Athena has once again made of things.

"G'way." Athena's tattooed arm takes a sodden, backwards sweep at the air. "G'way, stupid."

Her profile, smooshed into the ground, is a mask of vomit and dirt.

"All right. I will go away. I will go get something to wash your filthy face with. You disappoint me, Athena."

Athena's visible eye stays blearily fixed on the rooster.

Inside the dim, stifling hogan, Frances finds the one available cloth, her pink western bandanna. The only water she knows of is in the white plastic bucket. Biting her bottom lip, plunging her arm deep to wet the bandanna, she has to shake off the burred sleeve of flies. She stands quiet before the loom, an object of great dignity, a pursuit, elusive to Frances, of stillness and purpose. Hadn't she tried to make their marriage like that, into fine cloth, enduring design?

Balling up the tepid pink bandanna, wringing it hard, she squats behind Athena, turning her head and wiping her soiled

face. As she scrubs under her daughter's chin, a muddy back-
wash of rage hits.

"There." She throws down the stained rag. "You find something to do with that. I'm taking our things to the car. We're
going home, not that either of us has much of a home anymore."

As she finishes stuffing the trunk with their few things, Frances
hears the nurse, the one who had shown her the half-empty
whiskey bottle, behind her.

"Mrs. Waythorn, your daughter took off running that way.
If you take the car, you'll catch up to her. It won't be dark for
another fifteen minutes."

The woman's voice is nurse-like, so merciful, so profession-
ally equipped for trauma, Frances wants to collapse against her
ordinary sweatshirt, her calm and practical shoulder. She
wants to say oh you take care of this, somebody else manage
this, I only want to rest.

Even in the drought-smeared violet light, Frances easily makes
out the skinny speck of her daughter shambling along the gravel
and dirt road. In the middle of nowhere. Going nowhere.

As her car creeps closer, Frances, seeing Athena's set, miser-
able profile, does a most unexpected thing. She pumps hard
on the accelerator and shoots past her daughter, steering with
great angry lurches and radical swerves, up over the crest of a
small hill and down.

She stops, exhilarated, considering what she has done.
Abandoned her daughter. Gone beyond her. Swooped by. Yes.

The top of her foot has a dark wetted gash across it. Athena's potshard, the gift for her father, has rolled off the seat and smashed into pieces around her foot. Frances rests her forehead on the steering wheel. After a long while, she becomes aware of darkness. My god. She switches on the light overhead, lifts up to see the top third of her face in the little mirror. Smeared with dirt, tears, old mascara. Her pants, too, ruined. Her shirt, poisoned with uranium.

Wildly, she feels for the ignition, in a panic, shoves into reverse, backs up the car, coasts down the little hill she'd concealed herself behind.

Frances gets out of the car, sees blurrily, a mile or so away, the mercury yard light she had aimed for the night before. Hears, as if it isn't hers anymore, the sound of weeping .

The car light switched on, Frances is on her knees, searching under the seats, trying to gather back pieces of the clay pot. On the day she had been scrubbing down her child's room, on the day of her daughter's arrest, she had found, while on her belly under Athena's bed, a green cardboard shoe box. Inside were the souvenirs Frances had kept hidden from everyone. The dry, yellowish triangle of Athena's umbilical cord, a wavy, black shank of her ex-husband's hair, the auburn braid of her mother's hair, cut six months before she'd died, and like twin, eerie rattles, two tiny boxes of Frances's own ivoried baby teeth. Athena, searching through her mother's secret things, had taken, out of instinct or curiosity, all she needed.

"Ma-Mah? What is it? What are you doing?"

"My foot's cut."

"Poorest Mommy. You can't drive, bleeding and crying like that. Shh, shh, okay, shh. I'll help you. Shh."

Stripping off, wrapping the black tank top around her mother's foot, Athena, not bothering to ask, gets her old wish to drive. And as the desert night covers, uncovers her white, scarcely touched breasts, as her mother guards, unyielding, the broken potshards, Athena will piece together a stubborn, defiantly remembered, child's way home.